FORBIDDEN GIRL

BOOKS BY KRISTEN ZIMMER

The Gravity Between Us
When Sparks Fly

FORBIDDEN GIRL

KRISTEN ZIMMER

bookouture

Published by Bookouture in 2024

An imprint of Storyfire Ltd.
Carmelite House
50 Victoria Embankment
London EC4Y 0DZ

www.bookouture.com

ISBN: 978-1-83790-397-9
eBook ISBN: 978-1-83790-396-2

For you. Be gay, do crime.

Two families, the Calloways and the Monaghans, equally notorious, neither redeemable. Both have shed blood, vying for control of Boston's seedy criminal underground and all its dirty money. But sometimes there's an unexpected light in the darkness, a flame that burns brighter than hatred. And if the flame keepers are strong enough, they'll tell their families exactly where to fucking shove it...

PROLOGUE

JULES

The Meeting...

We gravitate around each other as we always have, two heavenly bodies locked in perpetual orbit, doomed to exist close together but never meet. Of course, I know of her. Rowan Monaghan is the stuff of legend. And I do recognize her. We don't run in the same circles, but today is a weird, one-off, Venn-diagram situation. Beyond that, she's hard to miss—like the North Star. It's something in the way she carries herself, as if she was born without any fucks to give. Hearing all the stories I've heard about her, it's funny seeing her doing something as mundane as blowing up pastel pink balloons with a hand pump.

"Jules, you can put the cupcakes over there." Rose points me to a long table adorned with a purple unicorn tablecloth, beside the ballon arch her cousin Merrick is assembling. I didn't realize what I was signing up for when I agreed to help with her seven-year-old niece's birthday party. *Why'd I volunteer to make four dozen rainbow unicorn cupcakes?*

I'm exhausted. I got home from school two days ago.

Adjusting to being back in my parents' house has sapped my energy completely. I haven't even finished unpacking yet. My mom tried to get my father to let me stay in Spokane for the summer; I'd arranged an internship at an investment bank downtown. One guess how that went. Dad prattled on about how Boston is an international trade hub and there were more opportunities for me at home than there would be in western-hemlock country, unless I was trying to grow Christmas trees for the rest of my life, in which case why the hell did he send me to college in the first place? He concluded his diatribe with, "I want my daughter home." Thus, fantastic as my mom is at schmoozing almost anyone into almost anything, her attempt was a failure. *Hemlock is also the name of a poisonous flowering plant. I don't think I'd mind growing those...*

As I saunter past Merrick with the plastic cupcake carrier, he breaks from working and whistles.

It stops me dead. "Oh, hell no, I know you did not just whistle at me." I speak in unison with Rowan, who asks him, "Did you just fucking catcall her?"

"Not at *you.* Not at *her,*" he replies in a panic, looking between us. "The cupcakes! Rose said you were making them, but they look like you got them from a bakery! They're really pretty and professional, that's all."

"Then use your words like a big boy and say that next time." Rowan purses her lips and squinches at him.

That look. I know they're friends, but there's murder in her eyes. I saw a mafia movie once where the main character said it's better to be feared than loved. I don't think it's simply a line from a movie—it's how she lives her life. I'm sure she gets that from her father.

Merrick ducks his head and says to both of us, "I was trying to be funny. Guess I failed. I'm sorry."

"Apology accepted," I tell him. Rowan nods at me, half-smiling, as if to say, *Thanks for forgiving this ignorant-yet-harmless fool.*

I smile back at her, then get busy stacking cupcakes. She and Merrick fall easily back into conversation, as if there weren't a heated exchange between them a second ago. "When does the kid get here?" I hear her ask.

"Two o'clock. Her friends should start showing up soon after. Oh, shit, it's getting late! We've gotta hurry this up. I have to change."

"Change?"

"I told Sammy I'd dress up as a green dragon for the party."

"You douchebag!" Rowan says so sternly that I quit stacking to look at them. She takes a quick gander around at everyone helping to set up. We're all in everyday clothes. The plan was to decorate the backyard and prep the food tables, then do a costume change before the birthday girl arrived. The disgust on her face tells me that she was never forwarded the memo. "You said it was fairytale themed. Why didn't you tell me it was a costume party?"

Merrick grimaces. "Because we needed a lot of help with the decorations and stuff, and I didn't think you'd come if I told you to wear a costume."

She stares at him, mouth slack. "Sure, I would have, dumbass! It's a kid's party. I don't wanna disappoint a kid. Work faster." She grabs a bunch of inflated balloons, moves to the arch, bends down, and starts fastening them to the bottom of the wire frame. My eyes are drawn to her backside, perfectly accentuated by her black slim-fit pants. I am Patrick Calloway's daughter; I shouldn't be thinking what I'm thinking about Callum Monaghan's daughter. And yet... *She's hot.* I choose to digest that as a fact, not a feeling: She is conventionally attractive, and her ass looks amazing in those pants. *Fact.*

"Juliet, what are you—" Rose says from behind me. She

follows the trail of my eyes. "Oh *no*. No, no, no. Get that idea out of your silly horny brain right now."

"Come on, there's no harm in looking."

"Except if you get caught looking by the wrong people, they'd gouge your eyes out. You know who that is, right? And who *you* are?"

———

And though I tried to resist, knowing exactly who she was, I couldn't help myself. The flirting became a first kiss, and before I knew it, we were playing a terribly dangerous game. One I'd never thought I'd play.

ROWAN

"My fucking fingers are killing me from tying all those goddamn balloons. Remind me to never do you a solid again." I pat Merrick's shoulder so he knows I'm messing with him. I was supposed to oversee the offloading of a shipment today, but this seemed more important. I pawned it off on Ben. One of the perks of being his boss; he couldn't say no to me. Not that he would have. Saturdays mean nothing to guys who are too eager to prove themselves to their higher-ups.

"How horrible for all the women loving women of Greater Boston. You'll have to take a night off."

I shoot him a sly grin. "I'd break too many hearts if I did that. I'll recover before the bars open tonight."

He chortles. "Atta girl."

He's still talking, but I'm mostly ignoring him. My attention keeps flickering to the table where Rose and the woman Merrick whistled at are arranging condiments. I can't place her, but I'm certain I know her. *How could I forget a woman who looks like that and is that audacious?*

She told Merrick off without so much as blinking. Standing up for herself like that took balls, even if she is acquainted with him. It's always a risk. Dudes have hidden tempers sometimes. "Who's the chick with your cousin?" I nod in her direction.

Merrick's smile vanishes in an instant, replaced by a troubled scowl. "Juliet Calloway."

Of course, *she's* Juliet Calloway. Somehow, that makes perfect sense. "Oh."

"Oh? That's it? 'Oh.'"

I shrug. "Yeah."

"You can't sleep with her."

It complicates things, sure. But I've never shied away from anything because it's complicated. Or dangerous. Or entirely idiotic. "Did I say I wanted to?"

He makes a circular motion in the air. "Your face says it."

"Maybe I'm interested in negotiating a peace treaty between our families, ever think of that?"

"Quit trippin'."

He's right. That would never happen. Anyway, I'm not interested in her for the potential diplomatic implications. She might legitimately be the most beautiful woman I've ever seen. Classic, like Grace Kelly. Which is twice as amusing because, as the only child of Patrick Calloway, she is also—kind of—a princess.

"Alright, I'm out," I say.

"Wait, what? Because she's here?"

He thinks I'm scared because there's a Calloway present? She's the least frightening member of that clan. On the face of it, anyway. "No, I'm leaving because I'm not dressed appropriately for this bitty bash, but I have an idea. I'll be back."

"What's the idea?"

"You'll see. Hint: You're a dragon, you should be very afraid of me."

"Dragons aren't afraid of anything!" he shouts at me as I'm walking away.

I yell back to him, "Neither am I!" As I'm leaving, I can't stop myself from thinking, *Bet I could get the Calloway Princess if I tried.*

And I did try. I told myself it was for the challenge. I didn't realize how much I had started to hope for more until it was too late...

ONE

JULES

"Stop right there, Juliet."

Damn it. I was hoping he wouldn't be in the living room. I know he's looking over his books, and that usually happens in his office. I back-pedal slowly across the open archway. What part of tonight's outfit could my father possibly find fault in? Can't wait to find out. "What's up, Dad?"

He gives me a once-over. "You look very nice."

It sounds like a compliment, but it's the start of a fishing expedition. I flatten the stomach of my lacey tank top like I'm checking for wrinkles, despite knowing there aren't any. "Thank you."

"You wouldn't happen to have a date, would you?"

Strictly speaking, no. But also, yes. I can't tell him that though. "I'm meeting Shannon and Rose for drinks." It's the truth, but not all of it.

"That should be fun," he says. Then he nods at Gino and Teague, who are sat on the couch opposite of him. "You two go with her."

"Seriously?" I fold my arms across my chest. It's a reflex,

ingrained at this point. "It's *Shannon* and *Rose*, not a summit of the mob families."

He lifts an eyebrow. "Tone."

"I wasn't taking one, I was stating a fact."

"They're coming with you, regardless. Monaghan's been busy lately."

Of course he knows that. Corporate espionage isn't solely for legitimate corporations. If it were only Gino, I could manage. But my cousin, Teague, is good at his job and takes it too seriously. He's elevated brown-nosing my father to an artform. "I'll take Gino. Teague should stay here and do math. He needs the practice." I stick my tongue out at him.

He laughs mirthlessly. "We didn't all inherit your intelligence, my smarty-pants little cousin."

"It certainly missed you, my shit-for-brains big cousin."

My father's face is stony as he says, "I said Gino and Teague are both coming with you."

I won't waste my breath arguing. I'd lose. Anyway, there's still a chance I could ditch them if I play my cards right. "Okay."

Dad nods. "Very good."

Neither Teague nor Gino seem to be in a hurry to get their asses off the couch. I'm not worried about being late. I just... *I can't wait to see her*. I tap my foot. My heels make an unpleasant *click-clacking* against the marble floor. Teague looks at me like he's dense.

"Well, can we go? God, Teague, it's like you only have two speeds: Slow and reverse."

That makes my father chuckle. "Best not keep the lady waiting."

At my father's behest, Teague practically jumps off the sofa. Gino, while the stoic type, lets slip a hint of annoyance at his overeagerness; I'm glad not to be the only one it bothers.

TWO

ROWAN

I check my watch for the time and notice the teal faux-leather wristband is starting to peel. *Have to replace it soon.* "Let's hurry this up, I'm supposed to get Elisa in half an hour," I call across the hood of the Jeep to Ben.

"Hold up, you're picking up El *and* meeting Juliet? That's cold."

"Did I ask for your input, Benjamin?"

Merrick snorts. He always does when I break out "Benjamin." I don't know what's funny about it, but he's a pretty simple guy. "You sound like his mom."

As I come around the car, I knock my shoulder into his. "My child would be much more handsome than this ugly motherfucker."

"Douchebag!" Ben says, but it's with a smile.

"Hey, Gallagher's right there." Merrick hitches his chin at a tall, gangly man in a Red Sox cap, standing at the top of an alleyway between two dilapidated brick buildings. Fucking Dorchester. What a cesspool.

"Stay here," I tell him. This could get messy and it's not his job to clean it up. Ben's the one on my payroll. I yell out, "Yo,

Gallagher! Just the man I was coming to find." The instant he clocks me, he takes off running down the alley. *He's really going to make me do cardio right now? Fine.* I kick it into high gear. Ben takes his cue from me and overtakes me almost instantly.

"Where you think you're going?" he asks. He reaches out, grabs a fistful of Gallagher's t-shirt, and yanks him backward— hard. I catch up to them in time to hear Gallagher making a choking sound, then move around him so I can look him in the eye.

I flick the brim of his grimy-ass cap and it rides up his forehead. "I'm only going to ask this once: Where's my money?" He doesn't have it. I know because he's terrified. I know he's terrified because his pupils are dilated to the size of quarters; he's a smackhead, his pupils are pinpricks most of the time.

"I have some but not all of it."

That's fair. Five grand is a lot to ask for from a middleman who uses more dope than he sells. "How much do you have?"

"Fif—fifteen hundred, maybe."

"Oh, Gallagher. My dad isn't going to be happy about this. You've owed him for too long." I take a glance around the alley. Propped against the building beside me, I find a rusty pipe with an elbow socket threaded to its end. I pick it up, give it a solid swing. It splits the air, sounding like a breath blown across the mouth of a glass bottle. "You like your kneecaps, right?"

The fear in his eyes spreads to the rest of his features. "Yeah."

"That's what I thought. So, here's what's going to happen. You're going to give me fifteen hundred dollars right now, and I'm going to give you until next week to come up with the other thirty-five hundred. If you don't, this pipe is going to become very well acquainted with the kneecaps you like so much. Do you understand me?"

If he were to piss his pants, I wouldn't be surprised. "Yes, I understand."

That's enough intimidation for one night. I don't like the taste of it. I drop the pipe. It clangs against the concrete, rolling across the alleyway until it meets the foundation of an apartment building. I give his shoulder a light punch. "Good man. Hand over the cash."

He digs into his left pocket, then his right, and produces two fat wads of crumpled bills. I should count it, but I have more important shit to do. "Let him go, Ben."

Ben releases his hold on his shirt. "Better run and find yourself a job."

He bolts with such speed, it's as if he sprouted wings out of his ass. When he's gone, Ben turns to me. "You can be really fucking terrifying sometimes."

Ha. "Thanks."

"So... Rapunzel's letting her hair down for you tonight?" he wonders as we head back to the car.

That's an inaccurate description of Jules. Essentially, she is a captive. But she wasn't kidnapped by a wicked witch; she's the seed of Voldemort. "If Calloway lets her out, yeah."

"Didn't her 'bodyguard' almost bust you two at the bar last week?"

"That was last week."

"You like living dangerously. *Too* dangerously."

He's not wrong there.

"Shotgun!" Merrick calls to Ben as we hit the top of the alley.

"Until we get El. Then your ass is in the backseat," I reply. "Manners."

"Right. Manners. Of course, *manners.*"

I roll my eyes at him. "Get in the car, wiseass, or forget riding shotgun, I'll strap you to the roof."

THREE
JULES

I never used to be the kind of person who was down for a Smash and Dash. I understand that's *en vogue* for my generation, but I can't think of anything less appealing than the chronic avoidance of genuine human connection. I mean, I enjoy sex, it's fun and it feels good, but how boring to not have to work for it. Make me earn it; I like a challenge. I think to myself *Rowan's never made me work for anything. It's always been easy with her.* From minute one. If anyone had to work for it, it was her. Probably harder than she's ever had to. I know her reputation: She's drowning in pussy.

I guess sometimes people do things that are out of character, against their better judgment or even their better angels. I wonder if that's what I'm doing now, propped up on the gold-filigree bathroom vanity, my back against the lighted mirror as Rowan presses her lips to mine. *It's only a Smash and Dash because we don't have any other choice. That's how we have to do things.* Still, this is risky, so public, and so soon after almost being caught. Worth it, though. It's been a long week without her. Keeping our distance was my idea. Worst idea ever.

"I missed you." She whispers it into my mouth as if she's stolen the words from me. She reaches up, moves my long, loose hair away from my neck—kisses, then licks my skin, sweet like sugar. The bite that follows is less saccharine, more bitter, lips and teeth and just a hint of pain, but somehow still sweet. It's everything I like about her in a single action.

"I missed you, too."

She glides her hands under my tank top and they creep into my bra. She massages my breasts, traps my nipples between her fingers, gives them a tiny pinch. Rubbing. *Mmm.* Another bite on the side of my neck, harder. Sucking. She goes for my earlobe and I have no more words for her to steal, only low moans. I can't take it anymore; I'm throbbing for her. I want her inside me, but she's not going to give me what I want until I beg. She gets off on the power.

She can have it. "Please, Rowan. *Please.*"

"Good girl." She nudges my legs open with her knee, runs her left palm up my inner thigh, up my skirt. Her slender fingers find their way into my panties, then into me—two to start with. If I want more, I'll have to ask nicely. Her left eyebrow raises, but it's involuntary. She's marveling at my readiness as she always does—not surprised, amused. It's no secret she gets me wetter than a Slip and Slide. She gets straight to work, thrusting deep, thumb teasing my clit, light and quick like the flutter of dragonfly wings.

Tonight, she's a bit rougher from the get-go than usual, more frenzied, but I like it. And I understand the reason. The Boston Harbor Hotel is neutral territory for our families, though I'm not here unsupervised. "The henchmen," as Rowan calls them, are waiting for me at the bar. Neither the round of fancy martinis I bought them nor chatting up Rose and Shannon will distract them for long. And the clock is ticking: The $100 bill Rowan slipped the washroom attendant only bought us fifteen minutes of the restroom being "closed for maintenance." It's not enough time. I want all night. I want to meet the sunrise with her arms around me. But this is all we ever get—precious pilfered moments. *Jesus, that feels so good.*

I don't want to waste another second thinking. I reach out, palm the back of her head and pull her closer. We're nose to nose and I'm panting into her mouth. "Kiss me," she commands, and I do. I give her lower lip a nip, and then my tongue is in her mouth, tangling gracelessly with hers.

I paw at her jeans and feel her muscles tense. She backs out of the kiss, although her fingers keep up their steady tempo. "Please, Rowan. I want to touch you," I murmur. She considers me, emerald eyes alight with awe. It's not something I've done before—not to her—even a month and a half into our clandestine rendezvous. She's always so attentive, so focused on making me feel good. She never thinks of herself. It's time for that to change. She is all I ever think about.

My legs are beginning to shake. I feel the heat rising inside me as my climax builds. "Slow down." I encircle her wrist. "Together, okay?"

There's an expression I recognize, devilish delight, transforming into something unfamiliar—submission. "Anything you want, gorgeous."

I'm barely able to contain my "thank you" as I undo her button, unzip her fly. She's wearing teal lace underwear. *Not such a tough girl, after all.* I swallow a smile at the thought and slide my hand beneath the waistband. *So smooth.* Further. I dip a finger inside her, discovering that she's already soaked just from touching me. Incredible. She seems like a two fingers kind of girl, so that's what I give her. And I use her wetness to massage her clit with the side of my thumb, matching her speed on mine. She starts to do that thing that drives me wild—fingers spread, drumming quick and hard on my G-spot. The moan I release is guttural. Feral. Her lips twist into a sly, knowing grin. "You fucking love that don't you?" she asks, a soft exhalation following each word.

"God, yes." Her confidence is so damn sexy. I have never wanted to give a woman an orgasm more in my entire life. I pick up the pace and hit my rhythm exactly right; her breath catches in her throat. She closes her eyes, chomps down on her bottom lip, and rocks against my hand. I can't tear my gaze away from her. The look on her face is delicious. Pure, unadulterated ecstasy. "You're so beautiful."

I can tell she's not used to hearing that and doesn't know what to do with it, because her mouth is on mine again, silencing me. Her tongue slips in, brushes my tongue. The way she kisses me—like she's been lost, wandering the desert for days, and my lips are crisp, cool water.

Her breathing is getting erratic. I feel her throbbing, the walls of her pussy clenching around my fingers. "I'm gonna come," she whimpers. I snatch her chocolate-colored ponytail, tug her head back. I want to see those stunning eyes overflowing with desire.

"Me, too." My entire body is quaking, edging closer to that moment. My muscles strain to the point of snapping. Hers do, too. And then it happens for both of us. It's sublime, the birth of a star and its collapse all at once. "Oh my God!"

"Fuuuck!"

She pulls herself out of me and rests her forehead on my shoulder. Her breath is ragged and balmy—warm, wispy ghosts caressing my skin.

I free my fingers from her body and lick them clean under her scrutiny. "I've been curious to know what you taste like. Have you been eating pineapple?"

She laughs close to my ear. It's loud and throaty, a sound I've never heard from her before. "I didn't realize you were such a top." She kisses my cheek and, without warning, drops to her knees. She looks up at me from between my legs. "My turn to taste you." She reaches up my skirt, bunching the sides of my panties into her fists.

I stop her. "You should probably get back to your girlfriend."

She sighs, the elastic snapping back against my hipbones, rises and nails me with those eyes, fierce and fiery. "She's not my girlfriend. She's who my father wishes were my girlfriend."

I watch her zip and button her jeans in one swift, sharp motion. She sidesteps me and turns on the tap, rinses away the remnants of me and dries off with a throwaway towel. We're not in the backseat of her Jeep or my BMW as usual, yet her routine is the same. She barely broke a sweat, but she'll still want to freshen up now that we're done. It's one of my favorite of her quirks, her fondness for cleanliness. It's why she always smells so good, like lavender mixed with vanilla.

"I'm not sure there's a difference," I say.

Her fieriness extinguishes in an instant. "You know there is, Jules."

I melt when she's like this, bare and honest, without the hard and proud mask her family taught her to always wear. I catch a glimpse of the affection she feels for me. Her eyes are glistening with it, even though she can't say it out loud. It's so forbidden it could get her killed; my family is just as hard and proud and violently screwed up as hers.

"I'm sorry. Yes, I do know."

"You'd better." And the mask is back on. "I'll leave first. Wait a few minutes, yeah?"

"Sure."

She heads for the door, and I think that's where we're going to leave it for the night. Until I see her shake her head, so slight it's almost imperceptible. She backtracks to me, takes my face into her hands, and kisses me. As she pulls away, she mutters, "I'm so soft for you, it's ridiculous."

That makes me smile. "Same."

"Nah, you're always soft." She winks. "I'll call you." She opens the door and then she's gone, returned to the real world, her friends, and the woman with the right last name who is, for all intents and purposes, her betrothed.

FOUR

ROWAN

"Yo, what the fuck, Rowan, you take a shit or something? You were gone for like an hour," Ben comments. I collapse into a chair at our table near the windows overlooking the dark water.

He knows damn well what I was doing, and I generally don't care how dirty his mouth is. Mine's worse. But I eye Elisa, who seems offended by my brash friend's filth. Her sensibilities are too delicate for Ben, Merrick and me. It's hard to keep my language in check around her, though I do try. She's not my girl-friend—in truth, I feel nothing for her—but she's still a person and deserves respect, regardless.

"How many times have I told you to watch your mouth?"

Ben's pale Irish skin flushes with embarrassment. He nods at Elisa, a poor excuse for an apology. Merrick smacks him upside the head, then says, "Sorry about him. He needs more training."

She waves him off and chuckles. "Boys will be boys."

"No, they will not," I reply. To Ben, I say, "Do better, bro."

He understands by my tone that I'm not playing. His gaze flits to the floor. "Okay."

Then I see Jules across the bar, making her way toward her

friends and the henchmen. She runs a hand through her disheveled blonde locks, smooths the hem of her black flare mini skirt. Her ice blue eyes find mine, but only linger for a millisecond. She really is dangerously beautiful, the kind of woman who, with nothing more than a smile, could get a man to leave his wife and kids. I'm ready to walk away from everything I've ever known, myself. Although it's not her physical beauty that has me by the balls, rather it's who she is: Intelligent—she's an economics major, for crying out loud—and kindhearted, which I realized the very first time I met her at that costume party. Someone's kid had tripped over his own feet and faceplanted onto the cobblestone pathway. She rushed over to him in her pink fairy costume, helped him up, hugged him, and whispered assurances into his ear until he stopped crying. Yet she still has a rebellious streak—that's obvious, I'm a symptom of it. What I hadn't realized until tonight is that she's also wicked funny. Pineapple!

The fact that she made me come in under three minutes doesn't hurt, either. That was mind-blowing. I should have let her fuck me sooner. I might have if she didn't give off such sweet, femme, bottom vibes. She has hidden depths and that scares me. I know myself—the deeper I dive, the more feelings I'll catch, and I can't afford that with the burden of my father's empire resting on my shoulders... and her father's resting on hers. She has me wishing that I'd been born into a normal family, had a father with a nine to five instead of the fucking kingpin I'm stuck with.

Merrick clears his throat. It tears me from my thoughts. "Here." I feel the butt of my Glock against my knee under the table. I almost forgot I'd given it to him before I went to the bathroom. Jules hates guns. I wasn't about to show up with it holstered to my back, for what finite amount of time I had with her. I take it from him, lift my button-down shirt from my waist, and secure the weapon in its discreet cradle.

"We should get going," declares Ben. "Fu—friggin' Italians get so cranky when they have to wait."

I check the time—10:42 p.m. They've already been at the dock for twelve minutes.

"He's right," Elisa confirms. "Frankie's temper is out of control."

That's because he gets high on his own supply. Idiot. Damn it. I don't want to deal with his whiny Sicilian bullshit tonight. I cover my angst with an eyeroll. "Your cousin will wait as long as I want him to wait, or he can drive down to Harlem for his snow from now on."

She smirks at me like she's impressed. Francisco Rossi doesn't scare me, and she knows it. He's got a big mouth and a flashy chrome Colt 1911, but he's nothing like his uncle. Or my father or Jules's. He doesn't have the stomach for real brutality. Alfonso Rossi wouldn't allow him to step to me, anyway. I'm supposed to marry his only child someday, solidifying the link between our two infamous families. And then the Rossi-Monaghans will own the entire eastern seaboard—guns, drugs, forgeries, everything and anything illicit. The Calloways will be small-time then, and my father's lifelong goal of crushing Jules's clan will be achieved. *The dickhead.* I snatch my Guinness from the table and chug it, slam the empty glass down so hard I'm surprised it doesn't shatter. "Alright, let's get this over with."

Ben, Merrick, and Elisa leave the bar first. I wait to steal one last glimpse of Jules, and it's like she intuits that my attention is on her. She flashes me that brilliant smile. I smile back, not giving a shit who may be watching.

FIVE

JULES

I don't think Rowan is the type to fall in love easily—or at all—but when she smiles at me like that, I second-guess that notion. And she did it with reckless disregard for the fact that Teague and Gino were observing her like a lab rat pumped full of a cure for cancer. Brave. Gross as it is, *I hate to see her go but I love to watch her leave* runs through my mind as she saunters out to the lobby after her not-quite-girlfriend. Rose leans in close to me and murmurs, "I know she's the first woman you've *really* liked in a crazy long time, but careful with that longing in your eyes." She motions a curt nod toward the bar.

I turn my attention to my overeager cousin and Gino. As if they'd have any understanding of what it looks like to be thirsted over by a woman. "Please. They're big, dumb ruffians."

She guffaws, and it tears Teague from whatever tedious conversation the men are in the middle of. He twists his lips at me, grabs his rocks glass from the bar and sidles over to our table, Gino a pace behind. He helps himself to a seat next to Shannon, gulps his whiskey, then asks, "Having fun?"

I was until you ruined it. "A gay ole time."

Rose snorts, but hurries to cover her lips with her hand.

I'd like nothing more than to be rid of him and Gino. There is a chance, small as it might be, that I can make it happen. It's worth trying. I can't stand the constant babysitting since school finished for summer break. Going to Gonzaga was the best decision I've ever made—I'd have left the country if my father would've allowed it. But Washington State is far enough away from his messy business that he doesn't feel I need protecting there. A sudden twinge of melancholy hits me square in the chest: Three weeks until I have to go back. *I'd trade my freedom for her.* I shake myself from the idea and concentrate on Gino. "Hey, Gino, you know we're supposed to be having a girls' night, right?" I sweep a hand across Rose and Shannon. "No offense, but you guys have all the wrong parts for that."

"Seriously," Shannon chimes in, "you're ruining the vibe."

Teague is the one who replies, annoyed. "Pretend we aren't here."

I sip my Malibu bay breeze through its orange plastic straw, then deadpan him. "Or you could actually not be here." His face goes sour. I ignore him. "Come on, Gino, the Monaghans are gone, the big, scary threat has passed. You've done your job for the evening. Don't you want to go home to your parents and little sis? You don't get to spend enough time with them when I'm in town and I feel terrible about it." That last part is not at all a manipulation tactic; I do hate keeping him from his family.

Rose, ever the dependable second, adds, "We promise we're not going to leave the hotel. Hey!" She eyes me. "Let's get a suite and stay the night." To Gino, she says, "That way you'll know where we are and one of you can come pick Jules up in the morning."

I can see Gino considering it, until Teague opens his mouth. "Your father told us to 'stick to you like shit on a shoe.'"

I know he isn't going to be swayed by my natural sarcasm. I have to be more tactful. Complimentary. Men are such simple creatures; all they need is a little ego stroking. *How pedestrian.* I bat my eyes at him, sad and adoring. "All I want to do is sit here, gossip with my friends, and relax. It's hurtful that you don't trust me—you, the closest thing I have to a brother."

At that, I watch him liquefy. He's always seen me as a younger sister, something fragile he's been charged with protecting. "You're relentless, Juliet, you know that?" he sighs.

I beam at him. He's going to let me have my way. "Yep."

He pushes his chair back, stands, and palms Gino's shoulder. "Right, twenty-two is old enough to be left on her own for a night." He points at me. "Don't rat me out."

"Never." I'm not stupid. We'd both be on the receiving end of Dad's wrath if I breathed a word about it.

His lips crumple as if he's doubting his decision. I deploy my puppy-dog pout. He sighs again.

"Night, ladies." Gino gives us all a cordial head bow.

Once they're gone, Rose throws her fist up for a bump. "Nice."

Shannon goes, "Smooth as warm butter."

I shrug. "I've had a lot of practice."

"Girl, we've been friends for a decade. Like we don't know you could teach the CIA a thing or two about the art of subterfuge." Shannon gives me an eyeroll.

Rose backs her up. "Like that time in high school you told your dad you were sleeping over at my place, and paid a homeless woman fifty dollars to pretend to be my mom, call him from my phone, and confirm it, only to go to Ryan's house and get wasted."

"His parents had good booze, okay?"

She chuckles. "You're a genius, Juliet, but one of these days your luck is gonna run out."

"Yeah, yeah. That day is not today." I signal to our waitress that I'm going to need another cocktail post haste.

SIX

ROWAN

"Tick tock, Monaghan," Frankie barks at me through his postnasal drip the moment we set foot on the dock. He has his gun out, waving it around like the tough guy he tries so hard and fails to be. His two backup thugs seem unimpressed by the display of toxic manliness.

"You have somewhere more important to be?" I respond. "And put your piece away." This is the part of the evening where we enter our usual power struggle stare-down. He doesn't like being told what to do by the "filthy Irish," or by a woman, and probably by a tried-and-true lesbian who has shut down his advances more than once. But I've got what he needs. He has zero leverage and he's well aware of it.

His shiny Colt glints in the wharf lights as he tucks it into his waistband. Subdued now, he gives Elisa a once-over and nods. "Hey, cuz. How ya doing?"

She purses her lips, not thrilled to see his messy ass, but she's polite, nonetheless. "Hi. Doing fine." Her smile seems effortless, though I recognize that it's forced.

I have no patience for him, either. I want to get this the fuck over with ASAP. Of all the things I hate about my job—which would be all the things—handling drugs is number one on the list. "Where's the cash?"

"Where's the shit?"

I turn to Ben, give him the go-ahead. He lifts the metal briefcase he's been lugging around all night and places it atop a blue plastic barrel, snaps the lock-clips, and pops it open. Frankie looks at the two perfectly wrapped kilo-bricks of blow like he's found his soulmate. It's the most pathetic thing I've ever seen.

"What's it cut with?"

"Do I look like I cooked it, you goombah? That's not my job, I'm just the transporter."

"Oh, you got jokes." He sneers, pulls a switchblade from his pants pocket and releases the blade. He cuts a small, thin line into one of the wrappers and scoops out a sizable mound of white powder, shoves the stuff up his nose, then sniffles. "That's *nice*." He goes for a second scoop and offers it to me. "Bump?"

"No, thanks." *You're the only braciola-for-brains on the pier tonight.*

He shrugs like *suit yourself*. "Give her the money," he says over his shoulder. The tall, bald guy in the navy-blue blazer comes forward. He plunges his giant hand into his jacket, fishes around inside, and pulls out a thick, folded yellow legal envelope.

Ben takes it from him, then undoes the clasped flap. "You don't have to count it," I tell him. His brow furrows. "Alfonso bankrolled it. We're all good."

"Pleasure doing business with you," Frankie says as he closes the briefcase. "You want a ride home, El?" he asks her pointedly, as though he doesn't trust me with her.

The nerve of this asshole. She's safer with me than she is with him. I'm less reckless than his showy self could ever be— not that the cops would give either of us shit, our families have so many of them in our pockets. But if he's willing to take her off my hands, I can ditch the guys and go back to the bar alone. "It's cool with me if you want to leave with him." I didn't want to take her out tonight in the first place. It was my father arranging our dates, per usual. It's always on nights like this one, when he's got some hardcore criminal errand he needs me to run. He thinks it'll be a bonding experience for Elisa and me if we share the culpability. And the guilt. All we have in common is the filthy lawless world we grew up in and he knows it.

There's a glint of dejection in Elisa's brown irises as she glares at me. I'm aware of how awful I am to her: I treat her like she's a colossal waste of my time, and that's by design. Maybe, just maybe, it'll be enough to get us both out of this predetermined clusterfuck if she's unhappy with me. She's a daddy's girl and regardless of how ambitious Alfonso may be, his daughter's happiness will always come first. The trouble is she kind of likes me, despite my indifference toward her. I'll have to try harder.

"Sure, Frankie," she agrees, demure. "You can drive me home." She steps closer to me, places the gentlest kiss on my left cheek. Reflex beats me at my own game, and I put my hand on her hip. She moves away, then runs her fingers through her long, jet-black hair. "Will you text me?" Her tone is so hopeful.

She's not made for this world. She's a wounded gazelle and I'm a ravenous lion. "Yeah."

She nods, satisfied as always with what little I've given her.

I watch her and the rest of the Rossis disappear into the blackness, then unclip the carabiner from my beltloop, remove my gun from my holster, turn to Merrick and hand him both. "Take the Wrangler and do... I don't care what, I need some me time."

He glowers at me, knowing that I won't be alone during "me time." I only ever part with my piece when I'm with Jules. He doesn't disapprove of her; he worries for me. It's not just Patrick Calloway and most of his family, there are a lot of people in this city who hate me because I'm a Monaghan.

"Can you keep your phone on? Your dad almost murdered me the last time I told him I didn't know where you were and he couldn't get ahold of you."

That's classic Callum Monaghan, control-freak extraordinaire. If it were anyone but Merrick—my best friend on earth and the only person I really trust—asking me to remain reachable, I'd throw my iPhone into the goddamn harbor. "Yes."

The guys depart and I'm finally on my own. I take out my phone, type a message to Jules.

My evening just freed up. I'll get us a room if you can you give the henchmen the slip.

I receive her reply almost immediately.

Already done. And a whole night together! Yes, please. See you soon. :)

Clever girl. I can't keep myself from smiling like a fool.

There's a gentle knocking on the hotel room door. I open it to find Jules shuffling in place like a nervous six-year-old at her first sleepover—which is half true, for us. It's the cutest thing I've ever seen.

"Hi." She moves to give me a little wave but then thinks better of it, which makes me grin. I check myself, and then check the hallway to make sure she wasn't followed.

"You gonna stand there 'til the sun comes up?"

She rolls her eyes as she steps through the threshold. I close the door behind her.

The very next second, she rushes me, slamming my back against the wall. She's got me by the collar and her mouth is more demanding than it has ever been. She's undoing the buttons of my shirt. My hands are on her ass, below her skirt. *No.* For the first time we *have* time, and we're damn well going to take it.

"Whoa," I say, still kissing her. I've never not wanted to kiss her before, but the inclination is too strong. I want it unhurried, the way she's always deserved it. I pry my shirt from her hands.

She looks at me, dumbfounded, lips twisted in a frown.

"What's the rush? For once we can afford to take it slow."

The thought hadn't dawned on her until I said it, but as it does her face lights with a quiet joy. "We can."

"Yeah." I push off the wall with my foot, usher her further into the suite. She's expecting me to lead her to the enormous king bed or the Victorian-style red velvet settee, and seems confused when I don't. I let go of her hands, strip off my shirt, and toss it on a chair, then undo my jeans and slip out of them. "Shower?"

"That sounds fabulous."

"Come here." I reach for her again, tug her toward me. She allows me the pleasure of undressing her and I do it methodically, my hands lingering on her skin longer than is necessary. When she's naked, it's my eyes' turn to linger. *If she isn't the most exquisite of all God's creatures.* I chase the thought away as I unclasp my bra, slide it off. Then my panties.

The water is scalding, so hot it could sear the flesh right off my bones. That's how I like it—painful, dangerous—as close to boiling as I can stand. I welcome the torrent as it rushes over me. But Jules is hesitant, standing at the open glass door, her nude frame somewhat obscured by thick steam. I must have a disapproving air about me, because she forces her doubt away and ventures in.

The stream hits her and her sensitive alabaster skin goes

instantly red. She winces but doesn't voice her discomfort. That won't do. I face the twin nozzles, turn the one marked *H*. The temperature change is immediate. "Better?"

"Much. Thanks."

I take her by the waist, wrench her fully under the water. Her blonde hair is soaked and spilling around her shoulders. I bunch it up, drape it down her back. "Don't thank me, just tell me what you need and you've got it."

Her eyes go wide at my words, as if she's never been more caught off guard by anything in her life. She doesn't speak, rather frames my face with her hands and kisses me gently.

Gentle. I don't know how to do that. I never have before. It's always been rough-and-tumble. Meaningless dalliances. I don't make love, I fuck. But she makes me want to learn. I deepen the kiss without urgency, guide her backward to the wall. I have her pressed up against the warm, wet tile, the tip of my tongue hinting to her lips that it longs to be inside her mouth. She accepts, and it's different from every other kiss we've had. Tender. More precious. I'm completely absorbed in her, like she is the only thing that exists in the world. Just her—her beautiful body and her beautiful soul.

With that I realize that I am well and truly fucked. Falling in love with her is going to be much too easy. I've already got one foot through the door.

I move my lips down her neck to her clavicle, savoring every inch of her skin. And then her breasts—each a perfect mouthful. I pick her up, support her slight frame with one arm and a bent knee, and it's the first time I've noticed how much smaller than me she is. By comparison, I'm built like a linebacker—tall and broad. *She's... Fun Size.*

She wraps her legs around my torso. My instinct is to get straight to the point, keep sucking on her tits, plunge my fingers into her, and work her pussy until she comes. It takes everything I have to fight against it.

I refocus on her mouth. She's surprised; I can feel her lips hesitate against mine, though it passes in a millisecond. I don't know what makes me do it, but I pull back. I need to see her.

"What?" she whispers.

Those eyes. "Nothing." I kiss her cheek. "I want you, but in the bed." I didn't say anything profound, so I don't understand why her expression looks otherwise.

"Then take me to the bed."

I cradle her in my arms, full princess carry, and back out of the shower, careful to dry my feet on the bathmat. She glances at the crisp white towels dangling on the rack as we're about to pass them. I think, *Fuck it.* I couldn't give a shit if we drench the sheets—and we will, one way or another. I'm not putting her down anywhere but that mattress, but I do stop long enough for her to grab one.

She dabs herself with it and sniggers. "Thanks." Then she kisses me again. It's a good thing I've had so many random one night stands here. I know this suite so well I can concentrate on her without worrying about crashing into anything. I sidestep the bar, avoid the low glass coffee table. Finally, after what feels like miles and miles, we make it to our destination. I place her on the mattress. She tosses me the towel. I stand at the foot of the bed, drying myself as I watch her scoot closer to the ornate gold bedrail and plump a pillow under her head. *How can someone be so sexy and so adorable at the same time?* I want to devour her. But tonight isn't just about me. *Give her all of you.* "What do you want?"

She's concentrating so hard on me it's almost as if she's seeing beyond my body, beyond my sinew and bones, directly into my heart. "I want you to ride my face."

It's such a straightforward answer, I don't know what to do with it. I'm usually the stallion, not the jockey, but I can't find the words to protest and don't feel like it, anyway.

I get on my knees, crawl up the bed, up her body—pause to kiss her before continuing on to straddle her shoulders.

She palms my ass and starts off slow, kissing and licking my inner thighs. The second her mouth moves into position, I'm electrified. Her tongue finds my clit and it's all swift flicks. I inhale the sharpest breath I've ever taken and, instead of air, exhale a whimper. That's all she needs to hear; she reads me like the *Sunday Globe* and starts to suck. I lurch forward, white-knuckle the metal headboard. It's all I can do to maintain my balance.

The shift in position allows her an opportunity she seizes with startling expertise. She sneaks her small hand into the space between my body and her chin and glides two fingers into me. Her tongue and her fingers move in cadence. I'm sure this is the closest to heaven I'll ever get. With every lick and stroke, my orgasm looms closer. I don't know if I'm way too easy or if she's way too good at this. Maybe it's both.

I must be too quiet; dissatisfied with my desperate panting, she goes harder, increases her speed. The cries I let out are not sounds I've ever made, just a melody I've enjoyed from count-less other women. "Fuck, baby, don't stop," I command as I lean back, slide my hand down her stomach and between her spread legs. "You're so wet." My words sound breathy, more a hiss than human speech. I use my middle finger to trace a circle on her clit. There's something magical to the whole "coming together" thing. Now that I've experienced the high, I'll be chasing it forever.

She flings her arm down, grabs my wrist. For a second, I think she's going to pull my hand away. Rather, she presses me against her, asking for more pressure without speaking. *Yeah, that mouth is busy.* She's moaning into me. I can feel her trying to concentrate on what she's doing but faltering as her own climax builds. I don't need her to work so hard; I'm almost there.

I start to ride her in earnest, bucking her mouth. Suddenly, I can feel the universe expanding inside me, white-hot and limitless. "Juliet!" I come so ferociously I swear my soul is shaking. And beneath me, she's quaking like her body is a fault line. I know she came, still I don't want to stop. Now she does pull my hand away, the action accompanied by a muffled, "Nuh huh."

"Guess you're done." I stifle a half-pant, half-laugh and try to dismount her with some modicum of grace, but my knees give way and I tumble sideways onto the bed. I'd be embarrassed if I had any energy left. I don't, so I just let myself laugh. She's attempting to ride out her quivering and catch her breath simultaneously. My crowing sends that effort straight to hell. She dissolves into a fit of her own. We're still a bit wet from the shower—from each other—naked as the day we were born and dying of laughter. I was wrong: I'm not falling in love, I've plummeted headlong into it. It's terrifying and wonderful all at once.

She wicks my wetness from her lips, then turns on her side to face me, still chuckling, and pushes my damp bangs out of my face. "I think this is the first time I've seen you with your hair down."

"No. That can't be," I reply as my tittering dies away.

"It is. You wear it in a ponytail most of the time, sometimes in a bun when you've been, um, working for your dad."

She's scary observant. "It's harder to grab when it's up. I learned after a couple nasty fights that that's an occupational hazard."

She runs a finger over the scar on my bicep that I got years ago from a shady motherfucker with a knife in Chinatown. There's a subtle shift in her mood. She doesn't like knowing that I've been hurt, or that it's pretty much inevitable I'll be hurt again. She's overcome with a kind of misty, opaque sadness, so heavy that it thickens the air between us. I want to obliterate it with kisses, refuse to quit until I'm sure it'll never distort her shimmer with its ugliness again. I go with my gut, sling my arm across her torso and pull her to me—kiss her until she's radiating that custom Juliet warmth once more. When I've finished and she's my Juliet again, I hold her. She presses her face into my cleavage, breathes me in. "Gerutwifme."

"Huh?"

She lifts her head and repeats, "Go out with me."

"Like, on a date?"

Her eyes narrow. "Yes, Rowan. Generally, when someone says, 'go out with me,' they're referring to a date."

It's not a foreign concept, yet I stare at her, agape. I can see she's starting to feel stupid for asking and wants to backtrack.

"It's fine if you don't want to."

Shit. "Don't be ridiculous. I want to. It's just... Do you really think we could go anywhere in the fucking Commonwealth of Massachusetts without it getting back to our parents?"

She recognizes that I have a point. I recognize that she has a counterpoint. "Who said it has to be in Massachusetts?"

Ha! That mischievous little simper. "You're kind of devious, aren't you?"

"I know how to work my dad's system."

I contemplate it. "I could swing it. My father isn't as protective of me as yours is of you. The real problem would be Teague. He's so far up your ass it's like he thinks he's a puppeteer."

Her hands fly up to her lips. "Oh my God, the accuracy," she says into them. She's chortling so hard that her eyes are watering.

I love her laugh. It's more boisterous than it should be—a noise too big for such a tiny frame. I could listen to her laugh every day for the rest of my life. "Alright, evil genius. What do you have in mind?"

She settles herself, nestles her head against my collarbone.

"*Mmm*. Maine. You and me in a tent on a beach in Maine for a weekend."

"Oh, a *weekend*, huh? That's a helluva date."

Her cheeks go rosy. "Yeah, that was presumptuous of me."

I'm not the outdoorsy type. And I'm surprised to find that she is. I'd never have guessed it by looking at her. But I like it, the sense of adventure I didn't realize she had until right this moment. Anyway, I wouldn't care where we went. If I get to be with her, I'm good. "Let's do it."

"Seriously?" Her big, blue eyes sparkle with enthusiasm.

"Yes."

"When?"

Now—no. Dad has a shipment of who-the-hell-knows-what coming into the harbor tomorrow and I have to be at the marina to receive it, or I'll get my ass handed to me. "This weekend. Will that be enough time for you to hatch an escape plan?"

She goes *pfft*. "Plenty."

I feel a bud of excitement in my chest. Mostly because I want to spend time with her, but also because it'll be nice to get away from the shitshow that is my life for a few days. "Cool."

"Cool," she echoes. Then yawns.

"You're tired. Let's go to sleep, okay?"

"Only if you keep holding me."

"Deal." I reach over and switch off the bedside lamp, then turn back to her. "Good night, Jules."

"Good night." She kisses my lips, then turns away from me and cuddles into my arms again, the perfect little spoon.

SEVEN

JULES

Rowan looks so innocent when she's sleeping, like she's never committed even a venial sin. But I've heard the stories. And I see her scars. She's taken blows and doled them out twice as hard. She's never killed anyone, though. Tough as she's been forced to be, she doesn't have that in her. She's had to steel herself to live the life her father chose for her, but I see who she is in her heart. I don't think she wants any of this any more than I do. Still, she's a better daughter than I am—defiant in her own way, yet dutiful; she does the jobs she's given without complaint, but also without joy.

I push her dark, messy bangs out of her face. She stirs, slowly opens her eyes. Those green irises focus on me and the thought that pops into my head is frightening. I'd like to be the first thing she sees every morning for eternity.

"Good morning," I say with a smile.

"Morning." She yawns. "What time is it?"

I check the clock on the nightstand behind her. "Eight o'clock."

"Hmm. We slept in."

I snort. "This is sleeping in to you?"

"I'm up with the sun most days." And then she does something unexpected: Leans into me and kisses my forehead. I try to curb the warmth from coloring my cheeks, but I'm sure it's pointless. "Sleep well?"

Very. "Yes. You completely exhausted me, Rowan Monaghan."

"I've been told many times that I'm exhausting," she smirks.

"Want some coffee?" I throw the sheets off me and move to get up, but she grabs my wrist.

"No, Juliet. Not yet. I want to hold you a while longer. If that's okay?"

"Of course it's okay."

She opens her arms for me. I crash into them, turn toward her, rest my head in the crook of her shoulder. She folds herself around me and it's startling how nice it feels, our bodies pressed together, all skin on skin. It's comfortable. Familiar, even though this is new territory for us. "Can we stay like this all day?" I ask without overthinking it.

"I wish."

As if on cue, her phone buzzes. Once, twice, three times. She doesn't move to pick it up. The caller takes the hint and hangs up. Thirty seconds later, it starts again. "Jesus fucking Christ," she grumbles, fumbling to grab it from the nightstand. "Sorry, I have to—" she says to me before answering the call. "Hey, Dad."

I hear her father, garbled, on the other end of the line, "Did you come home last night?"

I'm still resting my head on her shoulder. She grins down at me. "Nope."

"Should I take that to mean you had a nice evening with Elisa?"

Her grin vanishes. "No."

"I'd appreciate it if you'd try harder with her."

"Okay."

"Good. I need you back at the house by ten thirty. Can you make it here by then?"

"Yes."

"Alright. See you then." He hangs up. Rowan tosses the phone onto the mattress and sighs. I can feel the frustration stiffen her muscles.

I kiss her cheek. "How about that coffee?"

She lets out a breath and squeezes me around my middle. "Five more minutes of this."

"I wouldn't have figured you for a cuddlebug."

"I'm not. You just fit."

More buzzing. This time it's my phone. Rowan's closer to it. "Can you..."

She scrunches her lips to the side as she feels for my phone, then hands it to me. I sit up and hate doing it.

"Morning. No, I'm fi—Mom, you know me better than that, I only had two drinks. Tell him you raised a very intelligent daughter who is now a fully grown woman and—Oh my God, Mother, I can take the T. Alright, send Teague then, whatever makes Dad happy. Yes. Love you, too. Bye."

Rowan's looking at me, amused. "Is your mom always so wound up?"

"She's married to a paranoid mobster who treats me like I'm a genuine Fabergé egg, so, yes. She's not as frantic when I'm at school, though."

"Because nobody knows who you are on the West Coast. Juliet Calloway is your name, not your legacy."

She understands my position all too well; she might be the only other person on the planet who does. Is it any wonder that our connection is so singular and so intense? It isn't just sex. It was never going to be. The universe made sure of that. "Teague's coming to pick me up." I slip out of bed, over to the chair where the mixed pile of our clothes rests. Her eyes are on me as I dress, so I make a show of it for her.

"It's un-fucking-fair how gorgeous you are," she says.

"Look who's talking." I toss her panties to her. She hops out of bed, shimmies into them, and comes over to the chair.

Once she's fully dressed, she looks at me again. The corners of her mouth downturn in a scowl. "Well, it was fun while it lasted."

"Hey." I grab her arm and pull her close to me, then run my fingers through her dark hair. "You forgot about our Maine trip already?"

"Hell no. If you can make it happen, I'm in."

"It's happening. You'd better buy us a tent."

"I'll get right on it. One of those big, luxurious glamping ones for the Calloway Princess."

I chuckle at that. "I think Gucci makes one."

"Oh, you simply must have it. Nothing but the best for my love." Her eyes go wide and her mouth slack—panic combined with fear. Rowan had no intention of saying it, perhaps ever to anyone. It was a misstep, a slip of the tongue in a moment of humor. I want to make this easier for her, but I'm not sure if she's going to lean into it or try to take it back.

Her face turns stony. *I suppose there's my answer.*

"Shit. There's no point trying to run from it; it'll catch me." Rowan takes my face into her hands, rubs my cheekbones with her thumbs. "I love you, Jules. I didn't even know what that word meant before I met you."

The sincerity in her voice hits me harder than the words. I don't know that I've ever heard someone say it and really *mean* it, as though they've never been so certain of anything. "I love you, too."

I think she's going to kiss me. Instead, she envelops me in the tightest, warmest embrace, and it feels like I've found home.

———

Rowan sends me into the lounge to "sit down and enjoy a coffee" while she checks out with the concierge. I do as I'm told, mostly because I need caffeine, but also because, well, *Yes, ma'am.* I'm savoring the rich dark roast and the split view of the harbor and the street just as Teague's electric blue Mercedes comes to a screeching halt outside the hotel's main entrance. It's so ostentatious, I couldn't miss it, even if the grand foyer weren't made entirely of floor-to-ceiling windows. The problem with windows is they offer no cover; all it would take for the whole world to catch fire is Rowan turning around and my cousin catching sight of her. I send a hurried text.

Teague's here. Gotta go. Stay there.

I watch her retrieve her phone from her back pocket. Her posture changes as she reads the screen, spine straight and taut as a violin string. She texts back.

Good looking out. See you soon.

She leans against the high counter, and I head for the exit.

The doorman nods at me, grabs the long gold handle, and opens the door. I hit the pavement before Teague is out of the driver's seat. He usually opens the passenger side door for me like he's a chauffeur. It's kind of gross how hard he licks my dad's boots. "You got here fast. Just happened to be waiting for my father's beck and call?"

He slips his sunglasses up his forehead and nails me with a glare. "Are you hungover, little cousin, or did someone piss in your cornflakes this morning?"

I can't suppress my snickering. He's not good for much, but his comebacks are spectacular. "Neither. I'm not looking forward to going home, is all."

"I know. Hang in, you'll be back at school soon."

Don't remind me. "Yeah."

He guns the car onto Atlantic Ave toward Beacon Hill and my parents' house.

———

I manage to cling to the remnants of my good mood by my fingertips as Teague and I ascend the steps of the wide front porch, past the white marble Roman columns, and through the frosted glass front door. But I lose my grip on it the second I set sights on my dad. He didn't shave this morning and he wastes no time wagging his stubbly chin at me. "There she is! My daughter, the slippery eel, staying out all hours, no appreciation for the lengths I go through to keep her safe."

I close my eyes, take a breath, open them. "Dad."

"Don't you *Dad* me. You told me you were going to go out and have a nice time with your friends, then come home. But what did you do? You didn't come home and you conned Gino into leaving you alone, as if I wouldn't find out. I have half a mind to shoot him!"

"Dad!"

"And you." He looks past me and points a rigid finger at my cousin.

"Come on, Uncle Pat. She gave me the eyes!"

"I know all about those eyes, you little shit! And you should, too. You were damn-near raised in this house; you should be immune to them by now."

"Now, now, Patrick." My mother's soft voice streams into the foyer from atop the winding double staircase. She seems to glide down it. Effortless. Effervescent. Now and again, I can see the woman she must have been before she married a gangster. She wasn't always a nervous wreck; my father made her that way.

She rests a gentle hand on Dad's shoulder. "How could

Teague be immune to her when you're not?" She smiles at him, and it is magic. I see his anger melt away like ice cream in August. He's a bigger sucker for her than he is for me.

"Try to talk some sense into your daughter, please. Teague and I have business to discuss." He motions at my cousin to follow him into his office. I couldn't be more relieved they're both gone.

"Jules," my mother says. I know what's coming next. "Have you eaten yet?" It's the Italian in her. Food equals comfort, and her cooking always does.

"No."

"I'll make you some breakfast. Come sit with me in the kitchen."

That's an Italian thing, too. And even though my father is annoyingly proud to be Irish, that's one of my mom's customs he adopted; all the most important conversations in Italian households happen around the kitchen table. It's where I told my parents I wanted to go away to college. And where I told them I was gay. *Now I have something I can't tell them. Someone I can't tell them about.* The thought hits me like a sledgehammer wielded by a mugger I didn't see coming. "I'm not hungry."

"I didn't ask if you were hungry, *topolina*, I asked if you'd eaten."

Topolina. Little mouse. She hasn't called me that in a long time. There is no escape, so I shouldn't bother trying. I follow her through the dining room—the clicking of my heels against the tile floor grates my nerves more and more with every step—and into the kitchen.

"Frittata?" she asks, already in the fridge.

"Whatever you want. You're the chef." I take my usual seat at the glass table.

"With spinach and mushrooms. They're already cooked from dinner last night," she says, more to herself than to me, but I give her a nod anyway.

She makes quick work of mixing the ingredients in a bowl and heating a deep skillet on the stovetop. This is the quiet part. Well, the part where I'm quiet. She hums to herself when she cooks. I've always thought it was adorable. I use the silence to think up answers to the questions I know are soon to follow, but all my brain can conjure are lies.

I'm good at lying. Or telling half-truths, at least. All the most convincing lies have a hint of truth to them. My dad usually bites because he doesn't want to believe that I could be dishonest with him. I can never seem to get one past my mother, though. She can sniff out bullshit like a bloodhound. Sometimes she lets me slide, other times she pries. Today she's going to pry. I've given her good cause to.

She slides a plate full of egg concoction in front of me, along with a knife and fork, then joins me at the table. "So…"

And "so" it begins. "So?"

"How are Rose and Shannon?"

She's fishing. "They're okay. Shannon's going back to New York next week." *Truth.*

"Oh, Columbia's semester starts early."

Perfect set-up. "Yeah. She mentioned taking a girls' trip this weekend; her parents bought that house on the Vineyard last year." *Half-truth.* "Think you could convince Dad to let me go without the Garda following me?"

"That depends."

"On?"

"On if you tell me what's been going on with you. You're not normally such a 'slippery eel.' You used to like spending time with Teague and Gino, but now you seem bothered by them."

"I liked hanging out with Teague before he decided to work for Dad. Gino has a kid sister of his own to look after; it isn't right that he's stuck looking after me so often." *Whole truth.* Surprising.

"Alright. That's fair. But there's more to it."

"There isn't." I sigh. I can tell by the way she's looking at me that she's not buying it.

"*Mangia prima che faccia freddo!*"

"Okay, okay!" I slice into the omelet with my fork, take a bite.

"You've been disappearing without telling us you're going out," she continues, "and I've had to hear your father complain about it."

Another bite. Masticate. Swallow. Rinse and repeat.

"And when you come home from these secret outings, you're in a very good mood."

Because I've had multiple orgasms. "Is that a bad thing?"

"No, it's a fantastic thing." She gives me the Mom Look, that expression of clairvoyance, like she's an all-knowing oracle. "In fact, I'd quite like to meet the woman who's been making my daughter so happy."

I almost laugh. Almost. Because that's impossible. The more I think about the idea, the more impossible it seems. "Okay, fine. I am seeing someone. But you meeting her is not going to happen."

"Why not?"

"Because Dad would have a conniption," I let slip before I have time to take another bite of my food.

She smiles at me. "Do you remember how nervous you were to tell us you were gay? You got yourself into a fluster, tears and all. And after you did, your dad laughed and said, 'Of course you like women, who wouldn't?' He might surprise you again."

"No, Mom. This isn't the same. He wouldn't be so accept-ing." I drop my fork, listen to it ting against the plate. Then, without warning, the dam breaks and I can't keep the surge at bay. I don't want to keep Rowan a secret. I shouldn't have to, she's the person I love. "It really pisses me off because she's... She looks at me like I'm the only woman in the world. And she makes me feel that way, too—like I'm the only person she's ever felt safe enough with to let her guard down around. And she more than sees me, she *gets* me. In a way no one else ever has."

"That sounds a lot like love to me."

"I didn't say it wasn't."

"Then I'm not sure there's much your father could do about it."

I look at her like she's dense, as though she's forgotten who she's married to. "He's Patrick Calloway. He could do a lot about it." He's done plenty to put a stop to things and people he doesn't "appreciate," like holding a .38 special to my prom date's head, cocking the hammer, and threatening to blow his face off if he touched me "inappropriately" or got me home a minute past midnight. "I love Dad, but sometimes he can be one fry short of a Happy Meal."

My mother lets a small laugh escape her lips. "Good thing I'm not him, then." She places her hand over mine. "You can talk to me about anything, you know that, right? I don't tell your father everything."

"Can we just drop it? You called it, there's someone who makes me happy, and I have real feelings for her. Can't that be enough?"

"It can be. For now. I'll work on your father about your *girls' weekend*." She singsongs the last two words.

Technically, girls' weekend isn't a lie. "Thanks, Mom."

She pats my cheek.

EIGHT

ROWAN

I walk into my dad's study, hands in my pockets so he can't see they're clenched into fists, and take a seat in one of the well-worn brown leather lounge chairs. It's all I feel when I'm around him lately—restlessness, as though I'd rather pull a Forrest Gump and book it cross-country on foot than be in his presence, or do his bidding, or hear him speak. He doesn't have me in a stranglehold; my leash is long. But it's a leash, none-theless.

He's talking at me—I don't say *to*, because it's never *to* me—from his side of the desk. I'm not pretending to care, we're beyond that at this point, only pretending to listen.

I could've gone to college. I'm smart enough, and always got good grades. I thought about it for a while when I was younger, studying business management or something practical. Anything to give me a shot at normalcy, at going legit. But my father didn't think I needed to. "What are you going to learn about business management that I can't teach you?" he said, the one and only time I brought it up. "I've built you an empire. I'll show you how to keep it." Back then I didn't have it in me to tell him I didn't want it. I'm not sure I have it in me now.

If only I'd had a brother, the son he longed for who died alongside my mother in the delivery room when I was six years old. Then I wouldn't have to swallow this shit sandwich. And I probably wouldn't have been such a lonely kid, either. Someone else would know what his love looks like, how hollow and conditional it is. When I have a minute to think about it, I wonder if he's a sociopath, if he'd give a shit about me at all should I openly refuse to follow orders.

"Rowan, did you hear me?"

"No. Sorry, I'm pretty wiped."

"Well, do I know *this* girl?"

You sure do. "No."

"Hmm. Best to get it out of your system now before things get serious with Elisa."

Things will never get serious with Elisa. "You're right. So, you were saying?"

"Don't open any of the boxes at the marina. I just need you there to supervise and deliver them."

Like a felonious Amazon driver. Cool cool. "How many boxes are there?"

"Seven."

Lucky number. "And you're not going to tell me what's in them?"

"Do you want to know?"

"Not really." I'm sure whatever it is could kill someone, or a lot of people.

"It's safer for you if you don't."

"It would be safer for me if I weren't involved at all, but okay," I mutter beneath my breath.

He raises an eyebrow at me, folds his hands, and leans across the desk. "What was that?"

Shit. "Nothing."

He clears his throat, straightens his teal tie. *Nice color.* That's something I'll give the man, he's an impeccable dresser. I can't remember the last time I saw him in anything other than a three-piece suit. His eyes bore into me, green and intense—I inherited that gaze and those eyes from him. From what I can recall of her, the rest of me is all my mom. "Don't create a problem where there isn't one. Be there, keep an eye on things, and leave as soon as it's done."

"Okay."

"And don't take your Jeep. Alistair's Porsche is in the garage. Grab the keys from the rack on your way out."

Now I'm confused. "If Al's back, why am I—"

He slams his palms against the desk. "Just do what I'm telling you to do, goddamn it!"

If he were anyone else, I wouldn't let him get away with raising his voice at me for no reason. Parental privilege. "Can I go now? I gotta change."

"Yes. Call me when it's done."

"I will." I turn to leave, but only go a few paces before he stops me.

"Where's your gun?"

I run a hand over the empty holster at the small of my back. "In my car."

"Why is it in your car and not on you?"

"Because I had no intention of shooting the woman I was with last night?"

He lets out a sound that's sort of a laugh, but not really. "You never know who might intend to shoot you, though."

And whose fucking fault is that exactly? "Makes sense."

"I gave it to you to keep on you, so keep it on you."

"Alright." I nod and try to escape again.

"And bring that idiot friend with you."

He means Ben, not Merrick. Merrick's been my best friend since we were in first grade, and my father likes him so much he had hoped for a long time that we'd get married. The whole gay thing quashed that idea, but it worked out just fine for his grand plans in the end, with Elisa Rossi being into women and men.

Ben is Alistair's son. He's exactly two weeks younger than me, so we were brought up in this twisted circus together. Al was smart, though. He never wanted Ben to follow in his footsteps. Ben's a hopeless case, dying to make his bones regardless of his dad's best intentions. "I'll text him right now."

Meet me at the marina in forty-five. Cool?

He replies immediately.

Cool.

I hate doing shady shit in broad daylight. I feel so exposed. Not that it matters who sees what here; my father owns the Charlestown Yacht Club. It was a smart investment on his part —it operates like a legit business with members and dues, a fancy swimming pool and spa, a restaurant open to the public, a function hall, one hundred boat slips open year-round to any rich bastard who can afford it. It's how my dad launders his drug and gun money. He's a clever criminal. Today the dock area is closed for a few hours under the guise of dock repairs. Anyway, Tuesday mornings aren't peak business hours. I guess even wealthy people have to work.

I watch through the windshield as Ben careens into the marina parking lot like a NASCAR driver who just snorted an entire 8-ball of blow. I wouldn't be surprised if someday he narrowly avoids taking out a crosswalk full of children on their way to school, plus the crossing guard and a few parents. Windows down, music blasting, he drifts his Mustang into the open spot beside me.

"Hey, asshole"—I hop out of Alastair's Cayenne and slam the door harder than I'd intended—"this isn't *Fast and Furious*. You're gonna fucking kill someone."

"My bad, *Mom*."

"I will punch you in the face."

He smirks. "Why do you have my dad's car?"

That's a good question. "It's more spacious than my Wrangler."

"Must be a big haul."

I shrug. "You know I don't ask questions." Even though I should.

He nods. "Which slip is it today?"

"Sixty-nine." And before he can fall apart laughing like a teenage boy, I add, "Act like you've gotten laid before, you child." He contains himself and falls into step behind me.

There's a black 40-foot yacht waiting for us at the end of the slip. It's one of my dad's fleet, registered in the Bahamas to some shell company or another, an evil genius move if ever there was one. Two crew members are hitching it to cleats on either side and the captain, John, is overseeing them from the deck. "Hey, Rowan!" He hops onto the pier, then continues in his musical accent. "It's been ages. Look at you, you're all grown up!"

I smile at him, taking notice of the salt and pepper that's sprung up in his curly black hair since the last time I saw him. He's one of the few genuinely kind people in my father's employ. I bury the thought of what would happen to him if he were ever caught in international waters smuggling shit for my dad, and say, "Bring it in, old man." He wraps his arms around me and lifts me off the ground with a huff. I imagine this is how he greets his kids, with big papa bear hugs. *Must be nice.* We make some small talk. The weather in Nassau is hot and the tourists are insufferable. His family is doing well. Mine is... chronically unwell, but I say, "Dad's fine," then get down to business. "You have some cargo for me?"

"I do." He whistles at the crewmen. One jumps back onto the boat, the other positions himself at its side to receive. The first guy unloads a hand truck, the second sets it up. The process repeats seven times until the dolly is loaded.

"All set," he says.

"Great." I turn to Ben, palm open.

He looks at my hand. "What?"

"Empty your wallet."

"Why?"

"Because my father is your father's boss and that means I'm yours."

He pouts as he removes his fat billfold from his back pocket. As expected, he's carrying around stupid money, twenty-dollar bills in a purple bank strap, which he slaps into my hand.

I give the stack to John. "For you and your guys."

John's a proud man, not a stupid one. He doesn't argue. "Thank you."

I nod and say, "Take care of yourself."

John whistles again and the crewman pushing the dolly starts up the pier.

"It's the white Porsche. Make a right into the lot, first row," I call to his back.

Once he's out of earshot Ben whines, "That was two grand, Rowan!"

"I know. How many times have I told you not to keep that kind of cash on you? It's conspicuous. Get a bank account and debit card like a normal person."

"But they're traceable."

"Yes. However, the IRS doesn't give a shit about deposits smaller than ten grand. Stop being an idiot."

He shakes his head, but he's grinning. "Okay, lesson learned, *Mom*."

"Call me that again, I dare you."

"Mom," he repeats, then takes off running.

"You punk-ass little b—" I snicker and chase after him. I catch him at the top of the ramp leading to the parking lot, but rather than punching him as promised, I shove my fingers into the sides of his ribs. "Tickle attack!"

"Shit, no!" He swats at me. He's always been ticklish. And I've always capitalized on it to keep him in line. He's screeching like a little girl, and I realize as he grabs my wrists that he hasn't changed at all since we were kids. He's still the same dopey fool with the loud, annoying laugh. None of his bones ever turned mean. I have no clue why he wants to be a gangster.

Just then, a shout in the distance, *"Please!"* Both Ben and I turn toward it. I don't have time to rationalize or bark directions to him, my feet just carry me in the direction of the frightened shriek. I'm moving fast, faster than I've run in longer than I can remember. I toss a look over my shoulder and see that Ben is barely keeping up. Before I know it, I'm rounding the bend into the first row of parked cars. There's a gray pickup truck blocking Alistair's Porsche in its space, and a man is shuffling boxes from the dolly into its bed. A second man is pointing a gun at my crewman's head.

My instinct is to scream at the gunman, but on second thought that could startle him into pulling the trigger. Instead, I reach back and yank my gun from its holster. In one swift motion, I flip the safety off, aim at the guy's leg, cock the hammer, and pull the trigger. I never grasped how loud it is— the chemical reaction of gunpowder igniting, which forces a bullet from a barrel. I've shot guns before—a dozen times at the firing range—but I wore sound-dampening headphones then. Unhampered it sounds like an M-80, the deafening boom echoing all around me, off boats, and out over the calm water. And that smell... pungent, an odd mix of burned sugar and graphite.

The bullet hits its mark. The man yelps as a torrent of blood turns his dark blue jeans a sickly purple-red; the sight of it causes a surge of nausea in me. He drops his gun on the loose gravel and wraps his hands around his thigh. Ben thunders past me full speed ahead, undeterred by the sudden violence.

The other thief slams the truck's tailgate closed and hurries to help his accomplice, shoving him into the truck through the open driver's side door. Ben almost makes it to the pickup in time, but thief number two manages to scramble his way behind the wheel again. Door still ajar, he stomps on the gas pedal and takes off. Air resistance forces the door to close as the truck speeds out of the lot.

I catch up to Ben, who's already interrogating the crewman. Looking at him now, shaking with fear and adrenaline, it hits me that I don't even know his name. He's probably just some random day laborer looking to make a quick buck and John took him on for the voyage. He could've been murdered for a couple of boxes of who-the-fuck-even-knows-what.

"Are you okay...?" I ask, leading for his name.

"Damien," he says. "Yes."

"Ben, did you recognize those guys?"

"I didn't get a good look."

"Me either. But they knew we'd be here, so they must know who we are. Get Damien back to the boat. I'm gonna call my dad."

My father doesn't sound the least bit surprised to hear of the hold-up or the fact that I put a bullet in a man's leg. Cool and collected, he replies, "You did what you had to, don't worry about it. Did they get all the boxes?"

"What the hell, Dad? Did you set me up?"

"Don't ever say anything like that to me again. You're the only person on the planet I give a shit about. Now answer me, did they get all the boxes?"

Well, it isn't an "I love you" but it's as close as he's ever gotten. "All but one."

"Good. Open it."

I put my phone down on the hood of Ben's Mustang and rifle through my pockets for my folding keychain knife, forgetting for a moment that I didn't come here in my Jeep. Shit. Instead, I use Alistair's Porsche key to cut through the packing tape on the last remaining box and swoosh the flaps open. Inside I find tightly packed bottles of ibuprofen. My rage is unbridled; I yank the phone up to my ear and scream, "Are we trafficking for CVS now? Are you out of your goddamn mind? I fucking shot someone for generic Advil!"

He is unbothered by my anger. "We have a rat. Someone's been telling the Calloways when our shipments come in."

The Calloways... Panic climbs my ribcage like the rungs of a ladder. It could be me, however unwittingly. I told Jules I had to be here today. *No. She wouldn't.* "Do you know who?"

"I have an idea. That's why I sent you. I trust you."

"Who is it?"

"Alistair."

What? "Did you say—"

"Yes."

My eyes lock on Ben, his figure emerging from the dock in the distance. If his father betrayed us, my father will rain down his wrath on the pair of them. He's a follower of Shakespeare more than he is of Christ—the sins of the father are to be laid upon the children. "Do you have any proof? And are you sure it's the Calloways?"

"Yeah. The Porsche. They only target cargo I send Alistair to receive. He reports scuffles or that the goods were missing before he got there. There are never any problems for anyone else, just him. Days later the shit is on the market and Teague Calloway's the one hocking it."

I see. He didn't set me up, he set up Alistair—and Jules's family. He's going to start a war. This is the catalyst he needs. "Al's not back from his trip yet, is he?"

"No. He's still in New York with Celia. He parked his car in our garage, and I sent them in luxury, a nice stretch limo to a room at the Waldorf. I told them to take a few days, catch some shows, have some gourmet meals. There weren't any shipments on the agenda until next week, so he jumped at a vacation on my dime."

I think, *You dastardly no-good fuck*, but I'm not sure if I mean my father, Alistair, or both of them. If either of them could scheme to betray the other without a care... This game is ugly. I want out. I never wanted *in*. All the laws I've broken, all the violence I've done and been subjected to at my father's behest. And now there's a man—not innocent, but still a human being—somewhere out there with a bullet in his leg because I put it there. I know now, without a doubt, that I'm going to have to kill someone someday. Or I'm going to be killed. "I shot one of Calloway's men. I don't know who, it could've been Teague."

"That would be a problem. He's not just a hired hand, he's blood. Get home now. Bring Ben with you."

No! I am not leading the lamb to slaughter. I refuse. "Ben stays out of this, understand?" I'm shocked at my tone, so firm and unmoving. With that single sentence, I've jumped into perilous waters. I've got to tread lightly or risk becoming shark bait. "Our problem is Alistair, not his kid. Please, Dad. I've never asked you for anything, but I'm asking you to let Ben go."

He's silent for longer than a beat. My uneasiness swells with every passing millisecond. "Fine. Make sure I never see his face again. And if he causes any trouble—"

"He won't." I hang up without so much as a goodbye.

I turn around to find Ben posted up against a dock piling, arms folded—not impatient, simply waiting for instructions. Or an explanation of what the hell just happened, I'm unsure which. My heart is heavy, and it sinks further into my gut with every step I take toward him. My head dips instinctively. I can't look him in the eye. "I'm sorry, man. You're done working for us."

"What the shit? Why? Did I do something wrong?"

The bewildered sadness on his face makes him look like a schoolboy anticipating a scolding. I can't tell him that I'm saving his life. And I can't tell him that I don't have the power to do the same for his father. I could drop to my knees and beg at my dad's feet, my face soaked with tears, but he wouldn't be moved. A second who is disloyal to their first has no hope of salvation. Alistair knew that and he did it anyway. I take his hand, pull him to his feet and into a hug. In his ear, I say, "Ben, you're like a brother to me, so I'm forcing you out. Find a legit job behind a fucking desk or something, okay?"

He steps out of the embrace and looks at me for the longest while, trying and failing to suss something out. I'm careful to keep my face stony, give nothing away. "Yeah, okay," he says, suspicious. "Maybe I'll take a trip first. I've always wanted to go to Hawaii."

I guess he's not such a buffoon after all. "Excellent idea. But you'll need to get a goddamn bank account before you can book anything, Mr. Always Pays with Cash."

He rolls his eyes. "Okay, Mom."

NINE

JULES

My dad is sitting in his raggedy green leather recliner in the living room, reading an actual printed newspaper like the utter Boomer he is. I'm on the love seat opposite him, scrolling mindlessly through Instagram, happy to not be the focus of his attention for as long as I can manage. His trust in me is at an all-time low, as it should be. I'm keeping a sizable secret and I've been doing a lot of lying as of late to keep it. I wonder what the equivalency is: How many of the small white lies I've told throughout my life will it take to match one lie about the 5'7" gorgeous brunette mortal enemy I'm crazy about? And how long will it take for karma to catch up to me?

The front door flies open so hard that it smashes against the wall. If the glass weren't double-paned, it would have shattered. "Slow—ow, fuck!"

My father bounds from his chair and the newspaper floats to the floor. I follow him into the foyer. First, I notice the blood trail, a stark contrast of red against the white tiles, like a diseased little river carving through snow-covered land. Then I see Gino, with a pale hand wrapped around his gushing right thigh and the other arm slung around Teague, the only thing keeping him upright. My father doesn't get the chance to ask what happened; Teague spits, "The Monaghan bitch shot him!"

Oh, hey there, karma. Didn't take you very long. That is the last coherent thought I have. I know what I should do—help. Control the bleeding, call for an ambulance. But it's Gino, Teague's oldest friend, and thereby one of mine, too. Gino, who's a few years older than me, but whose shoes I always had to tie as a kid, who always covered his eyes at the scary parts of horror films, who used to chase the ice cream truck for Batman popsicles. Gino, who even as an adult greets me with unfunny knock-knock jokes, who wrangles Teague for me when he's around and sees I need a break from being Juliet Calloway.

Do something. Before I can act, I watch my father hurry through the archway into the dining room. He jerks a chair from its neat spot tucked beneath the table. "Sit him down." Teague helps Gino hobble over to the seat, and Gino collapses into it. "Go get a towel from the bathroom," my father commands Teague. I have never witnessed my cousin move so fast. He's back with a gray monogrammed guest towel faster than I can say "gray monogrammed guest towel."

My father tells Gino to, "Let go." Gino looks at him, confused. Once the directive clicks in his brain, he removes his hands from the wound. The blood flow increases. My dad ties the towel into a makeshift tourniquet. The silver C turns burgundy. In any other household I could pretend it was wine. Not here. This is not the first time the Calloway home has been turned into a bloody crime scene. I doubt it will be the last.

Gino's skin is pasty and he's sweating profusely. He might pass out at any moment. I'm no healthcare professional, but it doesn't take a doctor to tell he has one foot in God's waiting room. "He's lost a lot of blood." I bring up my phone's dial pad. "I'm calling 911."

"Do it," my father replies, his blood-stained hands shaking as Gino slumps against the chairback.

The call connects. The operator asks, "What is your emergency?" and I tell her in no uncertain terms I am watching a man die in real time from a gunshot wound that seems dangerously close to the femoral artery. She hurries through all the standard questions, double-checks the address, and dispatches an ambulance. I end the call.

I lock eyes with my cousin and realize he's shaking like my father, but not out of fear that Gino is about to expire—out of rage that Rowan may have stamped his best-by date. *Defuse him.* "I think this is the part where you tell us what happened, Teague."

He seeks permission from my father, who grants it with a nod. The story he recounts is asinine. I cannot fathom how Patrick Calloway, Criminal Mastermind, could be so incredibly stupid. And reckless. And outright warmongering. "I swear I'm going to kill her," Teague adds. He has a fire in his eyes. I know that expression. He means it.

Being hit hard by the initial shock of something is one thing, but panic is something else. It's not something I do. I'm a numbers person. I stay collected, level-headed in moments when others find it impossible to be. I see situations, calculate odds, and figure out how to twist them to my advantage. But in this moment, both logic and my talent for manipulation fail me. All I have is panic, because all I can picture is losing Rowan... In the ghastliest, most barbaric way possible—piece by piece. Fingers being mailed to her father. Her ears, tongue. Teague jokes that the T in his name stands for torture. I happen to know it's not a joke.

"So, let me get this straight. Dad, you sent these two miscreants to steal from the Monaghans, in the clear light of day on property they own, and now you"—I point at Teague—"have the audacity to blame Rowan Monaghan for protecting her family's assets, property and people. Is that right?"

Both men stare at me, agape. This is not a version of me

either of them has ever seen. *Take a good look, this is the Juliet you've created.* "Were you sending out an open declaration of war? What good did you think would come of this? Or did either of you *think* at all? Jesus Christ, thank God Mom isn't here, she'd be packing her bags!"

I have nothing left to say, and am uninterested in whatever retort either of them has to offer. I'm thankful for the blaring sirens of the ambulance. They grow louder as it approaches, until finally they go dead silent. Two paramedics charge in through the open front door, one with a large, bright yellow trauma bag in tow, and get to work on Gino. The taller, dark-haired man takes his blood pressure, while the shorter of the pair undoes the towel and examines the wound. I can tell by their expressions that Gino's situation is dire. Paramedic number two makes a splint above the wound to curb the blood flow. Paramedic number one asks my father questions. He's unhelpful throughout, answering with a steady stream of, "I'm not sure. I can't say. I don't know." I know better than to jump in and answer with the truth, but I have to force myself to keep it in. My dad's lies are never white, or even gray; they're black as death.

Once they've heard enough, they leave to retrieve a gurney, return and load Gino onto it with a synchronized three-count: "One, two, three." For some reason the taller paramedic speaks to me on their way out. "We're taking him to Mass General." He combs over my father and cousin. "In case someone wants to follow us."

"Thank you. I'll let his family know where he is."

I follow them out. They lift Gino into the ambulance, slam the doors, and start on their way. I watch from the doorway as the flashing red and blue lights disappear into the distance. When they're out of sight I head back inside and close the door behind me. Teague looks like he has something to say, but I speak first. "Save it. I don't care. If he dies, that's not just on

Rowan, it's on you, too. Both of you. Now which one of you wants to call his mom? That's not my job and I won't be doing it."

"I will," my father says. "Will you help Teague get this place cleaned up?"

"No. It's his mess; he can clean it. I'm going to my room."

All Dad does is shake his head in acknowledgment.

The only thought I have as I ascend the stairs is *I am so done with this family*. I close the door to my bedroom and take everything in—the soft pink walls, the white wicker furniture, the stuffed animals in their hammock suspended from the ceiling above my bed. Nothing about this room has changed since I was eight years old. That's how my father likes it, and how he thinks of me: As a child who'll go along with whatever I'm told to do or say. He doesn't know me at all. He doesn't want to. I don't want him to, either. What I want is to give up my name, this prison disguised as a home, my father's dirty money, and all the things it bought me that he convinced himself would make me happy. Nothing about this life makes me happy. I'm happiest when I'm three thousand miles away from it. And I'm happy when I'm with... *Oh God, Rowan!* I know she's okay, Teague essentially said as much, but I slide into her contact and hit *call* anyway. The line rings and rings and rings. I'm sure it's about to go to voicemail when: "Was it Teague? Did I shoot Teague? Is he alive?" The trepidation in her voice is palpable. I can picture her, racked with dread.

"No. It was a man named Gino. He was alive in the ambulance, but not looking too hot. I don't know if he's going to make it."

Her outbreath is hard. "Shit. I'm so sorry, Juliet. When I saw them holding a gun to a guy's head, I panicked. Now I realize I should have shot into the air or something. That might have been enough to scare them away."

"They were stealing from you."

"I couldn't give a shit about that if I tried. It's just stuff. Merchandise. Nothing is worth a person's life, not even the fucking Crown Jewels."

"They had their guns drawn and aimed at someone, Rowan. You did what you had to do."

"Don't say that. My father said the same thing, word for word. It's not true. I could have done something, *anything* else."

Whether Gino survives or not, she's going to carry this guilt with her for the rest of her life. I know there's nothing I can say to quell that, though I still want to try. I sit down on the edge of my bed, take a breath, conjure the memory of our first meeting at Sammy's birthday party back in May. How, after Merrick explained the costume-party part he'd left out, and they'd finished the ballon arch, she disappeared for a while. When she returned, she was wearing a knight's plated armor—steel, not the cheap plastic imitation from a party store. That was the moment I knew I had to talk to her, but she was so pretty and so standoffish that it took me another hour to get up the nerve. I learned that the costume was from a suit of armor that stood outside her father's study. And I learned who she was—I knew her name, her family's name, but that was the first time I saw who she *is*.

"Rowan, please stop blaming yourself for a situation you didn't create. You responded to it, that's all. Your protective instinct kicked in and reflexes took over. And you know what? I've known since the first time we spoke that you had it in you. That's why I've never once felt unsafe with you. You're caring and compassionate, and as much as your father may have tried to condition it out of you, he couldn't. I love you for that."

"Yeah?" It's a single, simple word, but I hear the astonishment in it, tinged with disbelief.

"Yes."

She sighs into the receiver. "Everything's fucked. This is the spark my dad's been waiting for. There's an inferno coming and it's going to be bad."

"I know." But how do we get out of the way of the flames? I'm not sure it's even possible. We'd have to disappear, and we need our own resources to do that, completely independent of and untraceable by our families.

"I gotta go. I think my dad's back from wherever the fuck he went. Keep me updated on Gino, okay?"

"I will."

She disconnects before I can say goodbye.

I don't want to be here but my desire to avoid running into my dad and Teague is stronger than my desire to flee. I grab a book from the to-be-read shelf of my bookcase and flop backward onto my bed, hoping to find relief in its as yet uncharted pages.

Screams rip up the stairs and down the long hallway, so loud and angry that they seep through my mahogany bedroom door and ring in my ears. I look up from my book for what must be the first time in hours—the sun outside my window is kissing the horizon with its fiery lips and the moon is creeping into the burgeoning night sky. I'd know that voice anywhere, though I rarely hear it this heated. The words are unintelligible, but my mother is losing her absolute shit. I run to my door, fling it open, and hurtle downstairs.

I reach the landing to find my mother in the foyer, holding the ensanguined guest towel so tightly in her left palm that her knuckles are white. My father is standing agog, no doubt wondering what the hell is happening with the women in his life. At the outset, I think she's pissed that her Very Expensive Towel from Saks Fifth Avenue is ruined. That's not it at all. The blood itself is inconsequential to her. She is demanding to know who it came from and why it is no longer in their body.

My father is, in a word, fucked. And he understands this perfectly. He stutters through the tale as he recounts it, shrinking with every word. My mother, on the other hand, seems to be getting larger and larger, until it's *Attack of the 50 Foot Woman* live from the Calloway Household Theater. "Patrick Calloway, have you lost your ever-loving mind?"

Up to now neither of my parental units have noticed my presence. "I asked him the same fucking thing," falls from my mouth before I can stop it.

My mother's eyes bulge as she acknowledges me. She doesn't normally take kindly to me swearing, but at the moment she's too incensed to care. "You've involved our daughter in this!"

"She was here when Teague and Gino arrived."

"It's not a secret, Mom. Dad's a gangster. Next question."

Neither of them is amused. "Juliet, go back upstairs. You don't need to hear this," my father says.

"I don't need to, I want to." I fold my arms across my chest. "Go on, Mom."

My mother takes a breath before refocusing her fury on my dad. "And where, pray tell, is your anger-issues-laden nephew? So help me, Saint Michael, if he goes after the Monaghan girl for this—"

"I sent him home to cool off."

I laugh. It's sardonic and biting and I can't help how it comes across exactly as I mean it to. "Cool off? He has *no* chill."

I've never seen a person hold a grudge like Teague. He could teach a masterclass on how to be irrational. How does my dad not know that? It's like he has no awareness of anyone or anything but himself and his own desires. He obviously doesn't ever take anyone else into consideration. *Selfish prick.* "Your dog needs a tighter leash." I decide that very second that I don't want to waste any more time or energy standing here, spitting into the wind. I turn to head back up to my room, then stop and face him again. His posture is that of a defeated man. My father being so impotent against the ire of his wife and daughter is a rare sight, indeed. I can use it to my benefit. And I'm going to. "I'm going away this weekend. I don't want to see Teague or any of your goons. I don't want you to call me a hundred times to check up on me. I want a quiet, calm weekend away from all of this."

He opens his mouth to speak. My mother's eyebrows narrow, and her mouth goes taut. She's daring him to argue in her Imposing Italian Woman way. "All I ask is you check in with your mother once in a while," he says.

"Fine."

Mom gives me a discreet wink. I grin to myself as I ascend the stairs.

I return to my book, trying to drown out my mom's hollering. It goes on for a bit longer. Then there's a sudden silence. She's run out of words or figured he's not going to listen to them anyway and given up. It's unfair that Gino is dying, and my father gets to continue risking other people's lives with little more than a stern talking to as punishment. For his henchmen it's fear, but for my mom and I it's love that keeps us loyal. He's a bad person. As an adult, I see that. But that doesn't erase two decades of him being a pretty good father, as far as fathers go. I never wanted for anything. I never felt unloved. I never wondered when I would see him again; he was always present. Still, I can't divorce who he is to the world from who is to me.

There's a knock at my door, followed by my mom saying my name.

I close the book, sit up straight. "Come in."

She starts with, "I'm sorry."

"You have nothing to be sorry for, Ma."

She shakes her head and sits down beside me on the bed. "I'm sorry that this is your life. I fell in love with your father even though I knew what my life with him would look like. I chose him. You never had a choice."

"You can't choose who you fall in love with, right? It just happens."

Her eyes lock on mine. "The woman who makes you so happy... it's the Monaghan girl, isn't it?"

Lying. I can't do it anymore. There's no point. "Her name is Rowan. And yes, it is."

She rubs her forehead. "Oh, you are your mother's daughter. In a city of a million people, you fell for the one person you shouldn't have."

"It can't work, can it? It's too hard. I should go back to Washington early, get ready for the new semester, try to forget her." My heart aches at the mere thought.

She knits her brow. "Yes, that is what you should do, but is it what you want to do?"

"No." What I want is to run away *with* her, not from her.

"Go away with her like you planned, if you still can after today. Talk to her. See if what you want is the same as what she wants. Whatever you decide, I'll support you, and I'll do everything I can to help you."

"You can't help me, Mom."

"Where do you think you got that big, cunning brain from, Juliet? Certainly not your father." She sneers and pats my thigh. "Well, it has been a day. I'm going to retire to the *boudoir*. Good night." She kisses my cheek.

"Good night."

TEN

ROWAN

I'm sitting at the kitchen island with my hands wrapped around a glass of water, staring at the blue and white backsplash behind the stove. I've been in this house, alone, waiting for my dad, for hours. He told me to hurry my ass home from the boat yard only to not be here when I arrived. If that isn't a metaphor for our entire relationship, I don't know what is. Physically absent he was not—just aloof, domineering, and completely uninterested in anything I've ever wanted or felt. So, I learned to take orders, to not want anything for myself, and to keep my feelings to myself. I'm a shitshow of detachment because he trained me to be. No, he tried to. He failed. Because Juliet is right, my cold-ness is an act. I don't know whether she's the first person who's ever seen through the hard-ass façade, or the first person to be brave enough to call me out on my bullshit, but it doesn't really matter. I've been discovered. My cover's blown. And I don't want it back.

"There you are." My dad's voice... I was so ensconced in my thoughts that I didn't hear the front door open, or the kitchen door swing on its squeaky hinges. Or maybe he's the Irish-American iteration of a ninja. I notice a brown paper bag in his hand. He tosses it onto the island and it skids to a stop just out of my reach.

"I've been here. Where the hell have *you* been?"

He squints at me. He doesn't like being challenged. I know that. But right now, I don't give a fuck what he likes. This is not the time to leave me hanging. He's the professional criminal here, and for the first time in my life I need his guidance. Shitty father, great mobster. He opens the refrigerator, grabs a can of Guinness, and takes a seat next to me. *Guinness. Dark and bitter and such a cliché.*

"Cleaning." He pops the tab and swigs the can. "I never thought Calloway would have the balls to send his own kid to rip us off. How interesting."

"Teague isn't his kid, he's his nephew."

"It doesn't make a difference; he treats him like his kid, he's as good as his kid." The evil glint in his eyes means he's acquired a new target. To most people, family is a source of strength. To him, family is a weakness, a tool to be utilized for a person's destruction. I never should've had any doubt: He is a sociopath. "He's a soft little man. Soft and stupid. This is all the excuse I need to hit him where it hurts, take out the people he cares about most and watch his whole life crumble."

He's talking to himself aloud as if I'm not a foot away from him. It's not something I've seen him do before. It makes him seem even more unhinged than I know him to be. The thought occurs to me that he won't stop at Teague. Juliet has always been far removed from the family business, but merciless is Callum Monaghan's middle name. She's unsafe, and neither my love for her nor my desperate desire to protect her can make her safe. She has to be someone else, someplace else.

I feel the rising tide of panic inside me. It must be plain to see because my father, never one for comforting, pats my knee. "You didn't shoot the kid, no worries. Just some upstart." And then his hand is gone from me and clenching his beer can again. He takes a long gulp. "Either way, he's dead—"

Dead. The whole world falls out of focus, goes hazy and dark like I'm the one who passed away. I don't process anything he says after that word; all I can hear is my own voice in my head spitting out synonyms for it: Deceased. Departed. Expired. Killed. Slain. Slaughtered. Yes, I did that. Me. I am a murderer.

Oh. There will be a wake. A funeral. A family mourning the loss of a son, a brother, maybe a husband and a father... And I can't even go to express my sympathies, apologize until I'm out of breath, fall to the floor and plead for forgiveness, for some measure of absolution. My mind conjures the kids I'm not sure Gino has, crying over his cold body, over the casket as it's lowered six feet into the ground, and in the future on birthdays, at dance recitals, graduations, weddings. So many tears for an absence that will always be felt and a Gino-shaped space that will never be filled. *Don't cry. You can't cry. He cannot see you cry.* "How do you know? How do you know he—"

"One of our cops heard, called me with the news." If it came from a cop, it's real. Official. There might even be a report on a desk in a precinct somewhere, cold, technical, scrawled with scientific words describing a corpse rather than a man. "You're a made woman now. Congratulations." Another swig of beer.

Congratulations! Like I achieved a life goal. And I did. His life goal for me. I'm ready to take over for him when he decides he's done. What is this feeling bursting in my core? It's not anger or sadness or guilt. It must be a twisted amalgamation of all three. I want to take him by the throat and squeeze until the life drains out of him. I want to watch the light leave his irises. But that won't fix things. Nothing will. I have to pay.

I leap up from my chair. He shoots his hand out and seizes my wrist. "I know what you're thinking. If you want to throw your life away over some nobody you whacked, that's one thing. But they'd try to use you to nail me. I can't allow that. Toughen the fuck up." There it is. The truth of who he is, laid bare: Self-absorbed, remorseless. And scared.

He'd deserve it if I ratted him out for every dirty deed I know about. But I'm not built that way. "So, you think I'd snitch. Am I as expendable as everyone else? You gonna kill me, Dad?"

He yanks his hand from my wrist as though I burned him. "I could kill anyone in the world *except* you. And no, I didn't raise a snitch, but that doesn't mean you'd never let anything slip. People fuck up under pressure. Even you."

"Then what happens now?"

"I took care of it so the cops can't tie anything to you. Still, there will be retaliation from the Calloways, which means you have to get gone for a while." He nods at the paper sack. "There's a hundred grand in there. Pack a bag and go. I don't want to know where."

"When and for how long?"

"Now and I don't know. It takes as long as it takes for me to finish what I've started. I have to clean house first, then I'll deal with the Calloways."

Alistair. Juliet. Ben. Merrick. All the people I stand to lose, in one way or another. Merrick is on the outskirts of all this, never in on anything I didn't bring him into, never with hands so dirty that he couldn't wash them; he'll be okay. Ben's a dope but not stupid enough to try to wriggle his way back in, so he'll be fine, too. Juliet is too big a problem for me to solve on my own; we need to work together on a plan. But Alistair... All it takes is a phone call. It's not snitching, it's warning. I owe him that. I owe myself that. I can't have another man's death on my conscience, and it would be—regardless of whether or not I'm the direct cause of it.

I crumple the bag of cash. "I pulled the trigger today and

ended someone's life. That's on me. But the way this all played out is your fault. I'm never going to forgive you for it. I would've done anything for you, without question, *except* kill anyone in the world."

He's never once shown an ounce of emotion. I've never forced him to until now. He grimaces as he says, "I know."

Maine. I'm going to a small beach town called Phippsburg, then on to a campsite on Hermit Island in the middle of Casco Bay. It's Jules's choice. She's never been there but says the white sand shimmers like diamonds in the sunlight and the water is warm and inviting, ideal for swimming. "Yes," I say, sans hesitation. She's going to meet me there tomorrow morning. We both need it.

She knows that Gino is gone from the world. I hate that I'm the one to tell her almost as much as I hate myself for being the one who took him out of it. I'm pretty sure I already know the answer to the question weighing heavy on me, yet I ask it anyway.

"Do you hate me?" I focus hard on her eyes through the FaceTime video. I know how sly she is, how effortlessly she can hide or bend the truth, but she can't keep the honesty from her eyes.

"Of course not. But I do hate that it happened, how it happened." Then she cries. Quiet tears. And at last, after years of not letting myself, I cry. No, I sob. Noisy and trembling. I don't know how long we cry together before we hang up, but I understand going forward things will be different between us. We both put our vulnerability on full display. Neither of us take that lightly. There's no doubt left that what we have is real.

I wipe my sodden face, collect myself as best I can, open my closet, all my dresser drawers, and start piling handfuls into an oversized duffle bag—things I might need and things I probably won't but would miss: Clothes, shoes, sundries, my phone charger, my favorite books, and the tiny Boston Red Sox beanie bear my mom gave me when I was five. It's the last remnant I have of her. I remember how much she loved baseball. All my memories of her are with her long black hair loose and topped with a Sox cap. My gun is on my nightstand. I'm bringing it, but only so I can chuck it into the fucking ocean. I shove it, and the cash, into my duffle, zip it closed, then pick up my phone again.

The line rings once. "Hey, kid, what's up?" Alistair sounds happy to hear from me.

I'm not happy to speak to him. As much as I care for him, he still betrayed my father, and trustworthiness is the one thing he instilled in me that I'm proud of. "Don't come back to Boston. Don't stay in New York, either. Take your wife and go somewhere far away. My dad knows you've been working with the Calloways and he's going to handle it the way he handles everything."

"Oh, Christ, Ben!" His voice shakes. That's how a parent should react when there's trouble: Priority number one, get the children to safety.

"He's out. I got him out. But make a plan for him to meet you in case my dad changes his mind. What the shit went through your thick skull crossing him, Al?"

"Callum is dangerous and getting more dangerous by the day."

"And Patrick Calloway isn't?"

"He's the lesser of two evils. He's hard, but he gives a shit about his people."

"Fuck 'em both. And fuck you, too." I hang up on him.

I take a last look around my room and it hits me that it was never mine. My father chose everything in it, even the color of the walls. I hate purple. I'd have picked teal.

I shoulder my bag, turn off the lights, and shut the door behind me.

Downstairs, my father is standing on the black and white checkered tile in the foyer, blocking my path to the front door. What else could he have to say to me? There's nothing left. We are unsalvageable. "I did the best I could for you."

He did his best? That's laughable. I'd have been better off if he left me on the side of a fucking highway to fend for myself. "Sure."

"I'll let you know when you can come home."

Don't bother. "Okay."

He moves in a way that makes me think he's going to try to hug me. I flinch. That's something I longed for, for years, a small show of affection. Not anymore. He steps out of the way.

I take the porch stairs two at a time. When I reach the side-walk, I turn around and stare at the brownstone, standing tall and bright against the dark sky over Commonwealth Avenue. For the briefest of moments, I contemplate burning it to the ground. To hell with Callum Monaghan. I am not going to be his voiceless pawn anymore. I don't care if I never set foot in this house, on this street, or in this city again. My life will be mine from this night forward. I flip the house—and my father—the bird, then head for my Jeep.

Interstate 95 is dark. I forgot how unlit the freeways are once you hit the North Shore. I swear I haven't seen a streetlamp since Somerville. My HD headlights do a good job of cutting through the darkness, and my Wrangler is a behemoth that could withstand a direct hit from a Russian rocket, yet for some unnamable reason I'm uneasy. It's a sensation I've had since leaving the Back Bay. Try as I might to rationalize, I'm failing. Something's off. I'm waging a war with myself to get good with the events of the day. There's nothing I can do to change the outcome, and maybe that's it: I feel unsettled because I am unsettled.

I glance at my sideview mirrors, left and right, and then my rearview. It's late on a weeknight so there's no traffic, save for a dark-colored Mercedes SL Roadster a few car lengths behind me. There's something familiar about it, which doesn't track—it's a very expensive model you don't see on the road too often, especially in Massachusetts; rear-wheel drive sucks in the snow.

I pull a quick sweep across four lanes, from the fast lane to the slow lane, then watch my rearview. The Merk doesn't sweep, but it does slink lanes until it's behind me again. *Unnecessary.* I pick up speed, sweep the whole roadway again. It follows.

I've been sharing asphalt with this car since Boston. I was aware of it but didn't think anything of it. Now it's undeniable: I'm being tailed.

I floor the gas pedal. The HEMI engine roars like a pissed-off lion whose slumber was interrupted; the Wrangler charges forward. Ninety, ninety-five, one hundred miles per hour. This bad bitch is made for off-roading, top speed of 120 mph. I can't outpace a Roadster built for velocity. I'm boxy, not aerodynamic, which means I can't outmaneuver it either, and whoever's driving the Merk is determined to stay on my ass. What's saving me is the distance between us, which is closing fast.

I read the highway sign.

EXIT 86, NEWBURYPORT/ROUTE 113, 2 MILES

Okay, I know Newburyport. I've delivered blow to some stupid rich people there. I decide to use the Mercedes' speed to my advantage. I slow down to seventy, then stomp on the brake. The Wrangler rattles as it skids to a stop a few hundred yards beyond the exit. The smell of burned rubber assaults my nostrils as the Roadster races past me. I throw the car in reverse, then gun for the exit, over the grassy knoll and curb that separates it from the highway.

Route 113 is even more sparsely lit than 95, another thing that works to my gain. I drive a few miles then turn left down a side street. I park the Jeep, grab my phone from the dash, my duffle from the front seat, and hop out. If I were dumping a car under normal circumstances, I'd take all the paperwork, remove the license plates, and file the VIN, but I don't have time for that if Mr. Hot Pursuit is trying to find me. I settle for the paperwork alone. The worst thing that'll happen is it'll get towed, and I'll have to retrieve it from impound.

Most of the cars in driveways and lining the street are unsuitable for what I have planned, late models with push-button starters and active alarms—not impossible, just time consuming—but at the far corner I find the one, a nineties Chevy Camaro. *Bonus, it's teal!* I peer inside, try the handle. The driver's side door is unlocked; no surprise in a bougie neighborhood like this. I slide in, pop the steering wheel column cover, locate the central wires, and get to work stripping their plastic coating with my keychain knife. Brown to yellow, battery to lights and radio, twist. The car's electrical system splutters to life. Add the red and green wires for the ignition and starter, twist. Gas pedal to the metal. *Vroom vroom. Fuck yeah!*

I handle the clutch, pop the gearshift into first and just like that, we're off. I'm in fourth gear before I even get back to the interstate. Speeding away in a stolen car has always been exciting. It'll never not be. That's how I know there are parts of me that will forever be untamable. Felonious. But street smarts aren't necessarily a bad thing to possess when you're in a bind. *Thanks for teaching me something useful, however messed up, Dad.*

I don't know who's driving the Mercedes, but there's no sign of them as I cross the border into New Hampshire. Twenty miles in, fifty miles in. Nothing. I want to call my dad and ask him about it. He knows, or can find out, everything. That was yesterday's solution to yesterday's problems. Today's problems are mine. Anyway, it makes no difference who or why. As long as I can outrun them, I'll be golden.

It's close to midnight when I arrive in Phippsburg. There are things I want to get done before Jules arrives tomorrow. If there's anyone who deserves a vacation, it's her. I might have ruined it, but there might be something I can do to save some enjoyment for her, and that means I need to get an early start. I find the closest hotel—a shitty Econostay—park the Camaro, laugh at how it fits right in with the rest of the beaters in the guest parking lot, and get a room for the night.

The mattress is hard as a slab of concrete, but it shouldn't be a problem. I'm so exhausted—mentally, emotionally, and physically—that I could sleep on a bed of hot coals. Tomorrow is going to be better than today.

ELEVEN

JULES

I come down for breakfast with a packed suitcase to find my parents at the kitchen table. My mother cooked a big spread, as usual, but neither of them seem interested in the food. They're silent as cadavers and just as stiff. Dad's staring at the refrigerator. Mom has her head in her hands. *They've heard the news.* I'm a magnificent liar but a terrible actor. I don't know how to pretend to be surprised that Gino's dead, or that I didn't cry myself to sleep last night after Rowan told me.

The most depressing thought comes to me: Maybe Gino is the lucky one. He's free now. Nobody can give him orders that put him in danger. Nobody can threaten him or hurt him anymore, and he can't threaten or hurt anyone else. Maybe that's what death is— freedom. From expectations and obligations and burdens and pain. But he'll never do or say or feel anything worthwhile again, either. He'll never laugh at another of my terrible puns or hug his mother or close his eyes at a gory scene in *Scream 15* or whatever-number sequel. He'll never have a family of his own. He'll never experience love, or joy, or possibility again. Soon, all he'll be is a pile of bones.

Fresh tears well up before I've been given my cue, so I

improvise. *Not such a bad actor.* I swallow the sob that's itching to be released from my throat. "Gino's dead, isn't he?" I ask my father.

His attention flutters from the distant nothing onto me. His eyes are bloodshot, as if he hasn't slept in a week. He hasn't lost an employee in a long time. No one's been foolish enough to take out a Calloway man in years. Well, the joke's on him. He's the fool.

"Yes, he is. He died last night. His mother called this morning."

I let the tears flow unrestrained. I'm sad, but also angry. He should still be here. It wasn't an unlucky accident that took him away. "He was twenty-six years old. How many more of your lackeys won't make it to thirty, do you think? And who will you lose next? Teague? Maybe it'll be me, targeted or caught in the crossfire, who knows."

"I will always keep you safe."

"How can you keep me safe when *you're* the danger? Your drugs and your guns and your heists and whatever other nasty stuff you deal in. You could've been a millionaire a thousand different ways, but you chose the ugliest way possible. Good job."

I've stunned him into silence for the second time in as many days. It suits me fine; I don't have anything left for him. I wipe my face and head over to my mother. She's crying. I wrap my arms around her, and she does the same to me. "I'm leaving. I don't think I'll be back for the service. I can't see Gino like that; it's not how I want to remember him."

"I understand." When I pull away, she looks at me like it's the last time she'll ever see me. Part of me would love for her to be right. "I love you, *topolina.*"

"Love you, too, Mom." This time, I kiss her cheek.

I don't say goodbye to my dad, just grab the handle of my

suitcase and roll it behind me. I'm out of the kitchen, out of the house, and in my car before I can feel bad about it.

I send Rowan a text letting her know that I'm on my way. She responds quickly.

> *Take Island Road all the way to the end. I'll meet you at Sand Dollar Beach.*

I type *Sand Dollar Beach, Hermit Island, ME* into my maps app. The drive will take two hours and forty-five minutes. That's too much time to be alone in my head. I need music or I'll go crazy. I open Spotify and Ellie Goulding's lightly graveled voice streams through the speakers. *Better*. I sing along with her as I start the car up the driveway.

The Sand Dollar Beach parking lot is sprawling and mostly empty, save a few cars here and there. Rowan is sitting on the remnants of a weather-battered wooden post, where the gravel meets the sand dunes, a western wind whipping her ponytail about. She looks small. And sunken. Somehow emptier than I'd left her at the hotel yesterday morning. Was that yesterday? It feels like a whole other lifetime. A lot can change in a day. Some people die, others take lives—unintentionally or on purpose.

She spots me, stands up, shifts her weight from foot to foot. Apprehension is a new look for her. I'm sure she's felt it before, but this is the first hint of it I've seen her display.

"Hey." She can't keep her gaze on me. Her focus drops to my rolling luggage. I relinquish my grip on its telescoping handle and cup her face with both hands. She still can't look at me, despite me trying to force her to.

"Look at me." She does. As strong-willed as she is, she finds it hard to refuse an order. There's shame and regret in her eyes. "What you did is not who you are. Understand?"

"No. But I understand it's not who I want to be."

"That's a start."

"Can you just... kiss me please?"

I'm startled that she asks instead of tells, because that's not her. She's too confident to ask. But I think if I don't kiss her, she'll cry. And I want to, so I do—soft and sweet so she can taste the love on my lips. She whimpers into my mouth. It's a one-note requiem. And then she's holding me so tight to her it's like we're standing in an undercurrent that might sweep me out to sea. Maybe she thought she'd lost me. Maybe she's thinking of all the ways she still could lose me. "I'm here and I'm not going anywhere."

She rubs her nose against mine. "What a fucked up beginning to our first real date, huh? And I had some dope plans in mind, too. It feels wrong to have fun now."

"It feels wrong not to. Gino was fun, always joking around and laughing. He never missed a chance to have a good time. So, can we try? For him. That's how I want to honor his memory. Okay?"

"Okay, let's try. First things first, take your shoes off." *Directions. That's better.* I slip my feet out of my sandals. She slips out of her slides. "Let's go drop your stuff off at the campsite." She grabs my bag with one hand and takes my hand into the other. As she leads me onto the beach, I think about how we've never even been out in public together before, let alone holding hands, and how nice it feels to be outside—with the sun beating down on us and the warm breeze licking our skin and her fingers laced between mine—without having to worry if anyone's around to see it. I want this to be what my life looks like, us together, not needing to hide.

"You look beautiful, by the way," Rowan says. "The sundress is very *you.*"

It's funny because it's true. I've had this pink floral print mini since high school. It's my favorite. And it'll never go out of style. "What, this old thing?"

"Yes, that old thing." She smirks.

The beach is deserted, which surprises me. Except in the distance, just out of reach of the waves at high tide, is a large tent. It's more of a yurt than a tent—a tall central pole draped with canvas. As we get closer, I notice the logos slapped across it: Gucci x The North Face. I turn to her. She reads my expression. "You thought I was kidding, huh?"

"You're ridiculous, you know that?"

"Maybe."

"How did you find this in *a day*?"

"Didn't you know there's a Gucci outlet in Kittery? A North Face one, too. I get shit done."

We walk past a firepit, two recliners, and into the tent. She puts my bag down at the foot of an air mattress, inflated, draped with sheets, and ready to sleep in. "This is a glampsite, not a campsite. Hold on, how is this all set up already?"

"It's amazing what DoorDash will deliver, and to where, and how willing people are to do manual labor when you flash a wad of hundred-dollar bills at them."

"Oh my God, Rowan, you sound like my father."

"Even a broken clock is right twice a day, but please don't ever say that again." She sits on the edge of the bed, reaches out, and pulls me down beside her. "If you want fun, I'm not sure how you feel about jet skiing, but we can rent one at West Beach."

"Are you a water sports person?" I just asked a woman whose family business is based out of a yachting marina if she *likes water*.

"There are multiple meanings to that phrase. Yes to one, no to the other." I roll my eyes and she grins before continuing. "When my mom was alive we used to spend Christmas vacation in Cancun. I don't remember much, but there are all these pictures around the house of us doing water activities—boating, jet skiing, snorkeling. I do remember swimming with dolphins once, though. The trainer was excited to have a pregnant woman in the water and told us that one of the dolphins was expecting, too. There was like, this natural bond that formed between my mom and that dolphin; she kept rubbing her snout on my mom's big belly. The whole experience was wicked cool. I'll never forget it."

"You've never talked about your mom before." *Or a sibling... Oh, Jesus, she doesn't have one.* "How old were you when she died?"

"Six."

"It's been you and your dad since then?"

"Growing up there was a revolving door of women in my house. I guess Callum Monaghan isn't quite forever material."

Everything about Rowan Monaghan makes perfect sense now, like looking at a Seurat painting from far away: Sure, you can tell that it's beautiful up close—the colors, the brush strokes —but its depth is unclear until you take a step back and get the whole picture. No one ever showed her that the most funda-mental aspect of love is staying, so she always runs. Even at his worst, my mom stayed with my dad because she always saw good in him. And there are pieces of him that are good. Very few people are all bad, although Callum might be one of the few. My father talks a big game and has all this swagger. He's beaten a few guys to within an inch of their life when "they deserved it," but I don't think he's ever killed anyone. I know Callum Monaghan has. It's common knowledge, and it's why he owns Boston. The city fears him. "I'm sorry. That must have been hard."

"It is what it is."

I can tell she's done discussing it. I glide my hand into hers again. "I like jet skiing. It's exhilarating."

"You've got a bikini on under that dress, don't you?"

"I do."

She's wearing black board shorts, a black swim tank, a sheer-white button-down shirt, and—my favorite part of the outfit—a white Red Sox cap, backward. She looks more relaxed than I know she actually is, and prepared to be in the ocean. "Here's what we're gonna do, jet skiing, followed by some chill beach time, lounging and tanning, an early dinner at a very fancy lobster restaurant in town, because we cannot come to Maine and not eat lobster, and then we'll come back here for sunset, a fire and some s'mores."

"I'm sorry, s'mores? You said the magic word."

Her eyes go wide with excitement. She points to a shopping bag resting atop a towel on the far side of the tent. "I got all the stuff; you wanna make 'em right now?"

Because I have functioning eyeballs, I've always known Rowan was sexy. Cute is a new discovery. It makes me smile. "No, we can save them for dessert."

"Alright. Let's move, we're burning daylight, and I wanna get my ass on a water motorcycle."

"A water motorcycle," I chuckle.

"What? That's what they are."

"You're right."

"There's something I have to do real quick. I haven't gotten around to it with all the preparations." She makes a sweeping motion around us. "But it's a need, not a want."

"Alright."

She kneels over her black duffle, back turned to me. When she stands again, I see she's holding her gun by its barrel. I loathe guns with all my being, and cringe at the sight of it, despite knowing that it's innocuous in her hand. She glances at it, at me. "I'm done with these fucking things. I don't ever want to own, hold, or even see one again in my life." She marches out of the tent like she's on a mission. I follow her down the sand, to the ocean's edge, and beyond, into the water, up to our calves.

She releases an empty magazine from the bottom of the gun's grip, then with her best impersonation of a big-league pitcher, winds up and throws it into the sea. She does it a second time with the body of the gun. The monstrous instrument of annihilation is swallowed by the waves. Rowan becomes instantly lighter, more like *my* Rowan. I think she'll be okay eventually. And I will, too.

"Now, water sports," she says.

"Water sports."

"Do you want your own water motorcycle, or do you want to share one?" Rowan wonders as she's looking over the jet ski rental board with pricing and time options.

"Mmm."

The young guy manning the rental kiosk overhears her. He gives me a once-over and flashes a smile. "You definitely want your own. You look like a girl who likes speed and being in control." He wiggles his eyebrows at me.

Gross. What a lame line. I was contemplating getting my own, but now I want to share one with Rowan. Besides, I like the idea of holding onto her, and of shriveling this bold bro's ego by making him watch me hold her.

Rowan slides her arm around my waist and presses her lips to my temple, then glowers at the guy. "Don't hit on my girl-friend. She's so far out of your league."

"Sorry," he mumbles, and walks away embarrassed under the guise of helping other customers.

I'm not taken aback by her possessiveness, or put off by it, either; it's kind of hot, and it means she's proud to be with me. But that word. So official. I wasn't expecting it. "I'm your girl-friend, huh?"

"Uh, yes? My bad, should we have processed that together first, like total lesbians?"

"What about Elisa Rossi? You're still seeing her."

"I was never seeing her. We've never been physical. We've been in each other's lives since we were kids, that's all. I told you, my dad had designs, but they weren't mine. And if you haven't figured out that I prefer blondes yet, what the hell's taking you so long?"

I kiss her. It's reactive. There are a hundred people on this beach, but I pay them no mind and couldn't care less if they pay us any, either. "Get one jet ski. You're going to let me drive it, though, right?"

She lifts her sunglasses and squinches at me. "I've seen how you drive on land. You'll be worse on the water. But fuck it, I'm prepared to go out with a splash."

TWELVE

ROWAN

"All I'm saying is people are scared of *me* when *you're* the danger to society," I say to Jules as I towel my sodden hair. We ate shit twice, neither time while I was steering the jet ski. "That last wipeout was nearly a whole-ass capsize, woman."

She's cackling maniacally, doubled over, arms across her bare torso. "You said you were ready to go out with a splash. I guess not."

"Thanks for introducing me to the horror the *Titanic* passengers must've felt."

"You're being dramatic."

"Am I really?" I grab her hips, pull her so close to me that droplets of salt water from her hair are dripping onto my chest. She's not laughing anymore, just staring at me with those gorgeous blue eyes. If I'm going to drown, it'll be in those pools. *Yep, dramatic.* "I don't know about you, Tiny Terror, but I'm starving."

"For food or for me?" She bites her lip. A knot forms in my stomach.

"Definitely for lobster. Sit your cute ass in the sun for a while and dry off so we can go get some." I drape my towel around her neck and saunter away from her, toward the rental kiosk and the cubbies where we left our stuff.

"That was rude!" she calls after me.

"Who's dramatic now?"

So far so good on the "trying to have fun" front, and she's as stunning as she's ever been in her hot pink bikini, wet skin glimmering in the late afternoon sun. I don't know why the thought of having sex with her is too hard to grasp at the minute. There's this idea gnawing at the back of my brain that I'm no longer worthy of being that close to her. I'm sullied, and if I'm not careful the hideousness inside me will rub off on her. A panicked, split-second decision and a small piece of metal stole my right to want that kind of intimacy with the woman I love, who somehow still loves me in spite of said decision.

It's fine for now, but it'll become a problem. And we have such little time left together before she goes back to school, thousands of miles away from me. She has to go, though. I don't want her to; I need her to. Whatever bloody shit my dad has planned for the Calloways, I can't stand the thought of Jules being anywhere near it. Maybe I'll go with her, change my name, get a job at a Starbucks or something. It's pretty fucking rustic out there, isn't it? I could live in a cabin in the woods or whatever. I'd be very happy with a simple, quiet life, as long as she's out of harm's way and coming home to me.

Jules's thin arms encircle my midriff from behind. She stands on her tiptoes to rest her chin on my shoulder. "You're stuck in your head, aren't you?"

"Kinda hard not to be." I'm replaying it in an endless loop. The blast of the shot. The cloud of smoke and scent of spent nitroglycerin. I can't recall if Gino screamed when the bullet hit him, but it makes sense that he would have: The eruption of bright red blood from his thigh, almost volcanic in force. It was arterial spray. That he survived for so long after is a wonder. "I keep thinking that if Teague had been smart enough or calm enough to take him straight to a hospital, Gino would be alive right now. Seconds count and he wasted too many." I lower my voice to a near whisper. "Or if I had dropped the fucking gun right then and there and taken him to an ER myself, regardless of what shitty crime boss he worked for."

"Okay, yes, you shot him." She lets go of me and steps around to face me. "Do you think someone else wouldn't have done the same thing? Gino would have. Teague would have. If it had been a cop facing down a man holding an unarmed man at gunpoint, they would have. That's America, Rowan. Bad guys with guns, good guys with guns, it's all the same. When everyone has one, everyone's on equal ground. That's why I hate guns."

I hadn't thought of it that way. "You're right, but it doesn't make me feel any better."

"You know what might? I know for a fact that if you weren't a Monaghan, and Gino hadn't been a Calloway man, the two of you would've been friends. He was a real tough guy, but only on the outside. He would've liked your sense of humor. You would've had him cracking up all the time."

That does bring a smile to my face. "Really?"

"Uh huh. Honestly, I bet my dad would like you, too. You make me happy, so my mom already does."

Say what now? "You told your mom about me?"

"She guessed. She's very observant. *Annoyingly* observant."

"She knew you were going to meet me, and she still let you come here?"

"Yes. She told me to. She gets it. She loves my dad and he's a total shitbag compared to you."

"Shitbag," I repeat. I can't stop myself from sniggering. "My old man, too. Shitbags, plural. Does that make us Shitbag Juniors?"

"I hope not." Jules sneers. "Come on. I'm dry enough and getting hungry. You promised me lobster; I demand you make good on that promise, post haste."

How she manages to be so forgiving and accepting, I can't understand. But it makes me love her more and feel even more undeserving of her at the same time. "Post haste? Alright, college girl. Let's post the fuck outta here with haste."

I grab her sundress and clutch from the edge of the towel. She relieves me of them, replacing them with her hand in mine.

"Babygirl, you wanna save some of that for the lobster?" Jules has melted butter all over her fingers, and a little dribbling down the plastic bib that was provided with her meal. "I heard tales of how graceful and elegant the Calloway Princess is. They were all enormous lies. Everyone back home is full of shit!"

"Don't believe everything you hear. I heard Rowan Monaghan was the most stone-cold badass bitch in the history of stone-cold badass bitches"—she leans across the table—"but it turns out she wears lace panties and likes to cuddle." She winks as she grabs her napkin.

The way she challenges me... She may be the only person I've ever met who has the stones to do that. I don't intimidate her in the slightest. Meanwhile, I didn't understand the concept of true fear until I met her. I never let anyone get too close—closeness, bonding, caring is risky. If I never cared, I could never be hurt by the loss of anyone. I care about her in a profound way —bigger than the word "lover" could encompass. There's a sense of duty to the way I love her. She's not a damsel in distress, and I'm not a knight in shining armor, but regardless of whether it's infantilizing or antifeminist or what-the-fuck-ever, I can't shake the need to protect her like we're living some King Arthur shit. We sort of are. It's the battle for Boston. I don't give a fuck about winning or losing it, but losing her would be intolerable.

Is this what all those cheesy romance novels drone on and on about? Finding someone who makes you feel whole when you hadn't realized you were half—until they walked into your life at a kid's birthday party.

Anything less than forever with her wouldn't be enough.

"Am I that big of a mess?" she asks.

"What?"

"You're staring at me."

"You are a mess. A perfect mess. *My* perfect mess, and I hope you never change."

Her head tilts, kind of like when a puppy sees something it's confused by. "You being so openly sweet is going to take some getting used to."

"*Pfft.* You like it."

"I love it. You're a complete mush for me."

"Well, you've seen me cry, so it's either be a mush for you or destroy you."

"Mush please."

"You got it." I take a handful of moist towelettes from the plate in front of me and slide them over to her. "For the love of God, use these."

"Yes, ma'am." She puts on an obedient face as she tears open one of the sachets.

People in Maine are unnervingly friendly, evidenced by how chatty our waitress is at the close of our evening. I'm used to servers checking in once during the meal, because that's their job, then handing over the check all careless and fake nice at the end. This woman asks questions: Are you here on vacation, where are you from, blah, blah. At my best I am not chatty. I have a shit ton of words in my head, though they rarely leave my mouth. Juliet, on the other hand, is a schmoozer. Charming and delightful. She could do this professionally. We complement each other in the best ways because we're opposites in all the right ones.

Jules says something cute about us taking a couple's long weekend. The waitress replies, "That's nice," and asks how long we've been together. It stops Jules. *Right. My turn.*

"It's pretty new, but when you know, you know." I place three hundred-dollar bills into the red check presenter and give it to her. "We don't need change." It's a nice tip for good service, but also a bribe to get her to go away. It's close to sunset and I was dead serious about watching it from the beach with Jules, a fire, and some fucking s'mores; my soul needs all of that.

"That's very generous! Thank you."

Yeah, yeah, I'm generous. Let me leave. "You're welcome. Have a good night."

We're up and at the exit *post haste.* I hold the door for Jules. She smiles to herself. I'm curious about what. "What's that grin for?"

"You're a badass bitch who opens doors and pulls out chairs. You must have learned that from your dad, so maybe he's not a total shitbag."

"I didn't learn that from my dad; he doesn't know anything about manners. I learned it from Alistair. It's how he treats his wife, and most people, actually."

Her smile disappears. "Alistair. I know him. I've seen him with my dad. I feel like I shouldn't have, though."

"You shouldn't have. He was my dad's right-hand." Now he's a dead man walking.

"Oh." It's all she has to say. She catches my meaning.

"I took care of it as best I could."

She takes my hand, gives it a squeeze, and keeps hold of it the whole walk back to Sand Dollar Beach.

· · ·

"Fuck me sideways, you'd think I'd be better at starting fires, right?" I'm frustrated by the tinder's stubborn insistence on not burning. I'm getting embers to spark, but it's too windy to light in earnest. Still, I'm leaning over the firepit, trying my damnedest. "Should've bought a Zippo."

I catch Jules as she looks up from reading the ingredients on a package of marshmallows. "Sweetie, it's a good thing. It means you're not an arsonist. Not being an arsonist is *very* hot."

I snap upright and drill her with a glare. "You just made a pun. You're punny. I'm dating a punster."

"Did I break you?"

"No, it's dope. And that one was awful. The worse the better." I snigger, and she does, too.

"It was really bad. Do you want help with that?"

"I thought about asking you to come stand over here and block the wind, but you're so scrawny it wouldn't help much."

She titters because she knows I'm right, but tosses a "fuck you" at me for good measure. "Come sit with me and enjoy the sunset. We can worry about arson and s'mores later." She thrusts her hand out toward me, fingers wiggling. I take it and join her on the recliners. "This is nice," she says. "The whole day was nice. Thank you."

"My pleasure."

We sit in silence for a while, listening to the small waves splash against the shore, and seagulls making their weird half-barking, half-honking sounds. I can picture us when we're old and gray, doing exactly this. I don't know that I've ever pictured myself living to be old and gray before. It's strange, but pleasant. I figured I'd be a brilliant star, one that burns white-hot for a short time then extinguishes unceremoniously. Maybe not.

"Hey, I wanted to ask you... Where's your car? I didn't see it in the lot."

Right. She notices everything. Now I understand she gets that from her mom. We have that trait in common, but mine developed over time for survival purposes. When your father uses you as a drug mule, there's a constant threat of attack or arrest—outside of the city proper, where we don't pay off half the police force.

If I tell her about the chase, how I had to dump my whip and commit grand theft auto, her mind will catapult into overdrive, tanking the chill vibe of the day. She's an overthinker, an over-plotter. She's too smart not to be. It's not information she needs. I lost the motherfucker, I'm positive of it. *Don't freak her out.* "I had an issue with it. I took a different one." Omission is not lying.

"Okay?" It comes out like a question, singsongy at the end. She could call my bluff or prod for more of the story, but she's content to drop it. "Just curious. You made it here, that's all I care about."

Thank you for letting it slide, my love. Sunset is past. The moon and stars are brighter here than in the city. We don't need a fire for light, although it is getting chilly. "I'm gonna try the fire again. I still want those goddamn s'mores."

"*Mmm.* Hard same."

THIRTEEN
JULES

"You're worse at eating than a five-year-old!" Rowan says with a chuckle.

"It's not my fault. You chose messy foods!"

"I did, yet I managed to not miss my mouth once."

"Touché."

"Conceding my point. Good girl."

She didn't say it in a remotely sexy way, but my body doesn't understand that. It's activated. *I'm too easy.* And she's too attractive. She has that beach hair thing happening, loose black ringlets cascading down her shoulders. And the flames are reflecting in her eyes, making them look yellow-green like peridot. And the top two buttons of her shirt are undone, so her impeccable cleavage is peeking out. And...

She reaches out to wipe a gooey glob of chocolate from the corner of my mouth. When she's done, I catch the tip of her thumb between my teeth, then take the whole of it into my mouth and suck. Her breath hitches as I release her. She trails her wet digit down my throat, then wraps her hand around it. The hint of a chokehold has me soaking.

She releases me. "I don't think I'll be any good tonight," she says, dejected. This is not the time to want her. We're both fragile in our grief. The world is off kilter. But the wretchedness radiating off of her...

I need to show her how loved she is, how deserving of love she is. "You don't have to be." I brush my lips against hers. Once, twice. By the third time, her lips are trembling. I pull back to see her fighting against tears. "Let me make love to you."

Nothing about her is submissive. She doesn't relinquish control. Even when following orders, she does it her own way. Rowan Monaghan takes everything and makes it *hers* entirely, me included. But she inhales the deepest lungful of air, and nods. I take her by the hand and lead her to the tent.

I undress her slowly. Sheer-white shirt. Black tank. Board shorts. She's fully nude before she reaches for the shoulder straps of my dress. I read her mien. She's pleading with me: *I need to feel your skin to be reminded I'm still alive.* I let her slip off my dress, my bathing suit. She touches me everywhere as she does, doesn't miss an inch.

She allows me to lay her down on the mattress. I lie on top of her. Then her fingers are tangling in my hair and I'm kissing her, tenderly, as if her lips are bruised. She accepts my tongue into her mouth. *She tastes like marshmallows and remorse.* I move my kisses to her neck, trace the hollow of her throat with my tongue. I massage her breasts, feel her nipples harden beneath my palms. Any other night, I'd pinch. Tonight, she'll be caressed.

She's starting to breathe heavily. I run my hand down her stomach, her pelvis. My fingers find her slit, wet and ready. She guides me to her clit instead. "Please," she mumbles. It's desperate, needy. Vulnerable.

"Okay, sweetheart." I use her wetness to tease her, soft and slow until she swells, then add more pressure and pick up speed. Now I know that she likes fast, firm circles right on the bud. I find the tempo that has her throbbing. It isn't long before her orgasm crests. She closes her eyes, starts bucking against my fingers and tugging my hair. Her abs go taut, and her thighs begin to quiver. Sweet little moans leach from her lips. *I could gobble up that sound.* I kiss her again, more fervently. She sucks on my tongue. Her screams of pleasure resonate in my mouth as she comes. I shift my weight off of her, let her breathe—I know she needs to.

She's like a different person when she opens her eyes again. They're fiery, not forlorn. "I want you to fuck me as hard as you can."

"What?" If we live a thousand years, those are not words I'd expect to hear from her.

"I need you to hurt me, Juliet."

"No."

"No?"

"If you want to fuck hard for fun, we can. But I'm not going to hurt you because you think you should be punished, Rowan."

Countless different emotions flash across her face in an instant. She wrenches me to her and, without warning, she's crying more fiercely than I fathomed a person could, her face buried in my chest, hot tears assaulting us both. She's shaking. I'm shaking. The mattress is shaking. I drape myself around her, like body armor made of flesh and bone. "I've got you," I whisper into her ear. I'll never let go.

———

Seagulls. Two of them at least, cawing at each other. Rays of sunlight stream into the tent. I'm holding Rowan. Her head is in the crook of my shoulder, her arm is slung across my stomach, and our legs are intertwined. I don't remember falling asleep. We must have crashed instead of drifting into it. Wakefulness slowly seeps into me, and I marvel at the fact that *I'm* holding *her*. I doubt she's let anyone do that before. Always the top, always in charge. I smooth her dark, bedraggled tresses. *You've met your match in me, darling.*

I get a few more quiet moments of playing with her hair before she wakes. She yawns, covering her mouth with her forearm. "I passed out."

"Me too."

She scoots away from me, plumps a pillow under her head. "Sorry for being such a mess last night."

At second glance, I see that the whites of her eyes are inflamed. I cup the back of her neck and rest my forehead against hers. "You don't have to apologize for having feelings and showing them."

"Not that. I'm sorry for asking you to do something I knew you wouldn't be comfortable doing."

"I don't mind getting rough once in a while; sex like that can be amazing. But not if either of us is in a bad place emotionally."

She kisses me, then turns her head. "Shit, I have lobster breath, don't I?"

"Don't worry about it. If you do, I do, too."

"Fair. Get over here and let me hold you for a while."

"Why, Ms. Monaghan, you downlow cuddlebug."

She sniggers as I curl into her. Once I'm settled, she trails her fingers up and down my spine so wispily I'd swear they were feathers. "What do you wanna do today?" she asks.

"Is this not an option?"

"It is, but there are others. We could go on a hike or a whale watching tour."

"Ooh, whale watching. I've never done that. There are seals here! I love seals. They're adorable."

"Seals attract sharks. I like sharks."

"Yep, that makes sense."

"That doesn't mean I don't like seals. They *are* adorable. Adorable food for great whites."

"I loathe you," I guffaw.

"No, you don't. You love me."

"I do," I reply.

She's austere all of a sudden. Something serious has popped into her mind.

I tap her temple. "What's happening in there?"

"You should catch the first flight back to Spokane. Get your mom to go with you if you can."

"Do we have to talk about that right now? Can't we just be naked together?"

"My dad is gonna find a way to bury your dad. And probably Teague. And whoever else is a minor inconvenience to him. I wouldn't be shocked if that means anyone who shares your last name. I thought about taking him out. Or paying someone else to do it. That'd be the easiest way to end this, save everyone. I can't, though. I hate his fucking guts, but he's still my dad."

"I know he is." I sigh. "I don't want to go back to school."

"You have to. It's the safest place for you. Anyway, it's your last year, right? You can't let all the hard work you've done amount to nothing. Besides, I wanna watch you saunter your gorgeous self across the stage to collect your diploma."

"It's not my last year, it's my last semester." The finish line is in sight. Four and half years, hours and hours poring over books, so many economic theories and mathematical models memorized. She's right, I can't quit. It would be a waste. "How could you come to my graduation? Assuming they're all still living, my dad, Mom, Teague, his parents, they'll all be there."

"I'll show up incognito in a hideous polka-dot dress with the ugliest permed ginger wig money can buy. God himself won't recognize me."

Ha! Even when Rowan's serious, she's funny. "I'd pay to see that."

"I could go with you. I'll get some plaid shirts, a few beanie caps, lean into that whole lumberjack lesbian vibe and fit right in."

I smirk at the mental image of her trading tailored button-ups and leather jackets for flannels. "As much as I love the idea of you being there with me, you can't give up your life to follow me to the other side of the country."

"What life? I don't have one anymore. I didn't have one in the first place. You and I both know that Teague is as bad as my dad. He'll try to kill me if I go back to Boston. I don't want him dead, but I'm not about to let him put me down, either. If we cross paths again one of us is leaving in a body bag."

The resignation in her voice is too absolute to argue. "You're right."

"I know I am."

"It's not as simple as you hopping on a plane to Washington with me. Do you actually believe your father will let you go? Or that mine will let me go? We are who we are; they'll always have their hooks in us."

Her forehead crinkles. She's getting irritated, searching for a solution to an unsolvable problem. "Then let's fucking change who we are! I'll give up my name; it doesn't mean anything to me."

"We could both change our names. Petition the court, pay whatever fees. But there would always be a paper trail. Social security numbers, bank accounts."

"You're talking about doing things the legal way, Jules. I'm not."

Of course, she's thinking outside the law. That's what comes naturally to her. She has a mind that functions on the periphery of societal norms. It's brilliant, the balanced footing she keeps between right and wrong, moral and immoral, light and dark.

"False identities?" I ask. "Do you know how or where we could get them?"

"Not yet. But with some time and enough cash, I could square it."

"That's the other thing. Money. Something like that wouldn't come cheap, would it? I don't have any money of my own. I don't even think my mom has her own; Dad controls every cent."

"I have money. There's a hundred grand in my bag right now, another twenty in a lock box at a bank that my dad doesn't know shit about. It's not enough to keep you stocked in Prada, but it might be enough to give us a fresh start." That last part she says with a grin; she knows I have expensive tastes, but don't need labels or fancy cars or a mansion to live in.

"Correct me if I'm wrong, but that duffle bag of yours is Balenciaga, no?"

"Yeah, and I'd toss it into the harbor like English tea if it meant I got to be with you." She squeezes me tighter to her side. "This is the wildest conversation I've ever had naked."

We both fall to pieces laughing. About how unbelievable our lives are; about how unlikely a romance like ours is to exist, much less thrive; about the unfettered audacity we both have to want it so badly that we'd do anything, give up everything, just to keep it.

"Jesus Christ, we're fucked," Rowan says once she's composed herself.

"Thoroughly."

"I'd like to stop *thinking* and just... go see some goddamn whales."

"That's the best idea ever. I'm one thousand percent on board."

"Good." She kisses me hard, grimacing as she pulls away. "For real, we need to brush our teeth."

And then, like two little girls playing in a park, we're laughing uncontrollably again.

FOURTEEN

ROWAN

I don't like the schedule, or the size of the crowd waiting for the next tour liner to depart. I see a middle-aged guy down the dock, mounting fishing poles to the back of a Stratos single-engine cuddy cabin boat, and am struck with an idea.

"Come on." I grab Jules's hand and steer her toward the slip. "Hey, man, how are you?" I ask the guy.

He looks up from his task. "Fine. You?"

"Good, thanks. I'm Rowan; this is my girlfriend, Jules." Jules gives him a little wave. He grins at her.

"Kevin." He thrusts his hand out for a shake, and I oblige him.

"Nice to meet you, Kevin. We were hoping to do a whale watching tour, but it seems wicked crowded. Any chance you do charters?"

"I do, but it looks like a good fishing day," he says.

Jules purses her lips to keep herself from smiling. *She knows me too well.* On the rare occasion I want something, I get it. She calls it my "can't stop, won't stop energy." She's seen it exactly four times: Right now with Kevin, once when a parking attendant tried to close up the public garage we'd parked in to have sex, the other day when I paid off the restroom attendant at the Harbor Hotel so we could have sex in the bathroom, and two months ago, the first time we kissed. She fought so hard against the longing, trying to see us as Calloway vs. Monaghan. I fought harder to get her to see us as Juliet and Rowan.

"How much will it cost to make it look like a good whale watching day?" I fish a stack of bills from the back pocket of my jeans. For someone who advocates bank accounts, I sure the fuck don't take my own advice sometimes.

"Um..." I watch him try to do math in his head.

Bro, just hit me with a number. It ain't rocket science. "A thousand for four hours sound fair?"

"Yes."

That was easy. He mumbles something about paperwork. I can't be bothered with any of that shit; I count out a grand and pass it to him. He examines the money, motions us onto the deck. I get on first, then help Jules on board.

He unropes us from the slip and it becomes evident that Jules does not have sea legs. She grabs hold of my shoulders as we motor away from the pier. "Oh, babygirl, *you're* not a water sports person."

"Correction, I'm not a small boat person. I'm a cruise ship person. Like, the city-sized ones big enough to have water parks on them."

I hug her. "Uh oh, no lido deck here. If you start to feel seasick—"

"No. I refuse to throw up."

"There's no shame in it."

"Rowan, we're Irish, yes there is!"

"That only goes for holding your liquor, silly goose."

"Silly goose?"

"I said what I said." It's disgusting how cute she makes me want to be, how safe it feels to embrace that version of myself when I'm around her. I guess that's what love is—feeling safe to be yourself with someone, all the best and worst parts of you, and trusting that they'll want it all. "Sit down." I guide her to one of the high-back bucket seats at the stern, leaning down to kiss her forehead before taking a seat beside her. "Your body will get used to it. But don't be a hero."

She doesn't puke. Twenty minutes on the water and she adjusts. Good thing, too, because I love boats. The family trips we'd take on one of my dad's yachts when my mom was still here were the days I was happiest. Happiness. I'd been without it for so long. It's nice to feel it again, however fleeting or clouded by my circumstances. In this moment, I am happy.

An hour into the tour, we pass a large colony of harbor seals lounging on a great rocky outcropping. It sends Jules into the most adorable flurry. She's pointing and bouncing up and down on the tips of her toes, going, "Ah, pups! Look at the pups!" She was cold in her jeans and t-shirt—I haven't seen her so dressed-down before—so I gave her my knit sweater. It's too big for her by a size and a half. The cuffs keep spilling over her hands, catching on her manicured nails, and it's starting to annoy her. "How haven't you grasped the concept of folding up the sleeves yet?" I take her arm into my hands and do it for her, creasing them up to her elbow. As I move to her other arm, I catch Kevin smiling to himself over it. *Alright. Fine. I'm cute. We're cute. It's fucking fine.*

"Whales!" he shouts at us and gestures to the horizon. About fifty yards off our portside we see dorsal fins, three of varying sizes, followed by three tail fins. Then, with unreal synchrony, all three animals breach the water's surface. Over and over. Full body. It looks like a dance—choreographed, fluid, and precise.

"Holy shit, they're gigantic!" Jules has her hands on her head as she stares in awe. "Humpbacks, right?"

"Humpbacks." I confirm with a nod.

"This is so much cooler than it is on the Discovery Channel!"

I pay more attention to her watching the whales than I do to the whales themselves. I've seen every species native to New England up close. Experiencing her like this, brimming with joy, is brand-new. It's so precious I could die. Her pure, child-like wonder is going to kill me. But I'll die happy.

I come up behind her and wrap my arms around her waist. She leans backward into me, rests her head on my shoulder. "Best day ever," she says.

I nuzzle her neck. "Best day ever."

"Sorry you didn't get to see any sharks," Jules says as we're walking back to Sand Dollar Beach. I've been too absorbed in the fact that we're holding hands—that she's swinging our arms back and forth the way a child would with a parent—to care about sharks.

"I'm glad we didn't. All those seals? Especially the babies. You would've been traumatized by the feeding frenzy."

Her features distort in horror. "I absolutely would have been, yes."

"You're so easy to get a rise out of."

"When you talk about baby animals getting eaten alive!"

I smirk. "Circle of life shit or whatever, it would bother me to see, too. Baby or adult."

She bumps her hip into mine. "As if I didn't know that."

The parking lot is fuller than it has been since we arrived. That's to be expected on an early Thursday evening in late July —lots of people are starting vacation or taking long weekends. I comb absentmindedly over the handful of cars. I see it, at the very end of the lot, half obscured by a line of trashcans: A blue Mercedes SL Roadster. I can't be sure whether or not it's the same one from the highway the other night—it was too dark to place the color and it never got close enough for me to catch the license plate number. However, it does have the familiar white and red Massachusetts plate attached to its front bumper.

Before I can stop it, my hand unconsciously grips Jules's tighter. Because she is who she is, she detects it, too. "Something wrong?"

I shift my focus back to her. *Maybe.* Probably not. How would they have found me? And two days later? I decide I'm being paranoid; it's my custom hyperawareness playing havoc with me. "Nah."

We stop to take our shoes off at the mouth of the beach and I check out the landscape. It isn't crowded, just two other tents, the occupants of neither tent in sight. The only company we have is a flock of sandpipers chillin' at the water's edge, waiting for the changing tide to wash in some hermit crabs. I have that weird, unsettled feeling in the pit of my stomach again. Trusting my intuition has yet to steer me wrong. The closer we get to our tent, the more intense the sensation gets. My gut is screaming at me to turn around and run as fast and as far as I can. I slide my left hand up my back to where my gun used to live in its holster. It's a reflex that'll die hard.

Jules also senses that something's not quite right, but is more confused about it than I am. Every step she takes is hesitant, guarded. Is she feeding off me or can she feel it, too? I should've told her the truth when she asked about my Jeep. My decision to let her remain unaware might be putting her at risk, and I'm unarmed. She regards me with questioning eyes. All I can do is shrug. "Stay behind me," I mutter. As cunning as she is, she's a hundred pounds soaking wet and not made for physical alterca-tions. She understands that as well as I do, so she does as she's told and falls out of step with me.

I open the tent flaps with caution. My stomach churns as

the inside comes into view. There, sitting on the edge of the inflatable bed we didn't remake this morning, is Teague.

"Fuck."

"What?" Jules asks. She looks around me. Her hand goes clammy in my palm. "Teague? How did you—"

He grabs her rose gold iPhone, holds it up, waves it around. She hid it under her pillow so she'd be forced to spend the day living in the moment instead of through a lens. "You forgot to turn off Family Sharing." All the calmness in him drains away. He springs to his feet and roars, "I fucking knew it! I fucking *knew* it was her when you defended her to your dad and me! How long have you been fucking her, you traitor? Even now, after she killed my best friend!" He's stomping toward us like a sasquatch on speed. I wish I hadn't gotten rid of my gun; there's no doubt he's packing. He lifts his shirt and sunlight glints off the silver finish of a 9mm.

I don't have time to think—I let go of Jules's hand and charge at him. When I'm close enough, I kick him hard in the chest. The sole of my foot connects with his sternum. It knocks him off balance but not on his ass as I'd hoped. He regains his equilibrium before I can kick him again. His gun is in his hand. As he moves to aim it, I throw a vicious southpaw with all my weight behind it. It nails him in his left temple. I hit him with a one-two punch combo. Same story, both sides of his head. He reels from the impact.

I hear shouting from the tent's entrance. I grasp that it's Juliet, but I can't make out her words. And then she's rushing at her cousin, shouting, "Teague, stop! Please!"

It happens in an incomprehensible blur: I'm unsure whether she runs into him or if he intentionally smashes her with the barrel of his gun. The force of the blow is such that she falls to the ground on her side. When she pushes herself upright, I see that her right eyebrow is split open. She's bleeding. Copiously. No. That wasn't an accident; he pistol-whipped her.

Kill him.

I've always known I was fast, though not this fast. I hurl myself at him full speed and launch a high kick at his wrist. I hear the sharp snap. He shouts in pain and hunches, grasping at the small, now-broken bones that connect his digits with his arm. He loses his grip on his gun and it hits the ground with a thud. Leave it or pick it up? *Fuck it, I'm gonna murder him with my bare hands.* I yank him upright by his damaged wrist. He yelps like a little bitch. I plunge my knee into his balls, then let him collapse to his knees. Once he's down I kick him again, this time connecting with the underside of his chin, right at the top of his throat. His head lolls backward and he goes down harder than a piano dropped from a fourth-floor window.

He's lying semi-motionless on his back. I'm not sure he's conscious enough to understand my words, but I say them anyway. "Yeah, you're such a fucking big man, huh? Getting your dick handed to you by a girl." I crouch on top of him, tug his short blonde hair, turn his head toward Jules. "Look at what you did to your cousin!" I scream, inches from his ear. I punch him again. And again. Blow after blow to his face, ribs, face again.

My knuckles are getting sore, and they're coated in his reddish-purple blood. I know I should stop beating him, but I *can't* stop. It's definitely him or me, and probably him or Jules. I will not let it be her. There will be nothing recognizable left of his face when I'm done with it. I crack his nose at the bridge. His left eye socket concaves.

"Rowan, no!"

Jules is standing over me, pleading. "Your dad's still your dad. Teague's still my cousin." I stop mid-punch to glance up at her. My rage evaporates at the sight of blood from her wound mixing with her tears.

I stand up, winded. Exhausted. My body is getting heavier as the adrenaline rush fades.

Teague is barely breathing. He'd be dead now if she hadn't intervened. I splutter out, "He shouldn't have touched you." I have no explanation beyond that. And I can't say I'm sorry for going savage on him, because I don't think I am. I can't find it in me to care a single iota. Maybe I'm a rabid animal and the best, safest thing for humanity would be for someone to put me to sleep.

"No." She touches my shoulder. That single touch is all it takes to bring me back to myself. She's the water to my fire. I'm a livewire and she is my grounding.

I glance at Teague, watch the shallow rise and fall of his chest as he struggles to take in air. "Shit. I really messed him up." I wonder if I crushed his windpipe with that kick to his throat, cringing at the notion. "I don't know where that came from. I like, snapped. Because... he did *that*." I gesture at her gash.

She presses the butt of her thumb to it and winces. "Yeah."

I rush to my bag, dig through it for a clean towel. "Hold this to it." She's going to need stitches. And there's literal blood on my hands: A man panting for his life on the floor of this tent. Despicable as I know he's capable of being, I don't want to be *him*. I walk over to the mattress and snatch one of the pillows from it. Carefully, I raise his head and slip the pillow under it. The elevation helps alleviate his struggle for oxygen, but it's not enough. This time around, I won't make the same mistake. Jules's phone is lying next to Teague. I palm it and dial 911.

A man's voice on the other end of the line gives me the familiar cop-show spiel.

"I'm at Sand Dollar Beach on Hermit Island. There's a man here who's hurt badly. And a woman who's hurt, too. I need an ambulance right away."

FIFTEEN

JULES

There's a small audience gathering outside our tent to ogle the spectacle—me receiving butterfly bandages to hold my gaping eyebrow closed, and Teague being loaded onto a stretcher. The EMT gathers he has a broken wrist and nose, and a fractured eye socket. One or two of the lower ribs on his left side are probably cracked as well. I hear my cousin groaning in pain. I stare at the tracks left behind in the sand as he's wheeled away. I should be upset that he's suffering, that Rowan hurt him, just like I should have been upset that she shot Gino. But I'm not. Gino was an unintended casualty of our family feud. I know how heartsick Rowan is over her actions, and how deeply she wishes she could get a do-over. Teague is a casualty of... being a sexist douche who solves everything with brutality, of thinking he could take a woman half his size without a problem.

I'm sitting in one of the recliners. Rowan is standing beside me with her arms folded, gnawing on her bottom lip, shifting between looking at her freshly cleaned but battered knuckles and following the gurney with guilt-ridden eyes. This life of violence is too much for her. It's too much for me, also, but I haven't lived through it first-hand until today. Thinking of how this is routine for her makes me sick to my stomach. Thinking of how Teague would have shot her, and maybe me, in hot blood, and felt zero remorse for it, makes me furious.

An EMT is leaning over me, checking my forehead for fractures. I shoo her away. "Please stop touching me, I'm fine." She pulls her gloved hands back as if I'm holding a knife and demanding she give me all her money, then packs up her bag and heads for the ambulance. "Do you still have my phone?" I ask Rowan.

She grabs it from her rear pocket. The first thing I do is turn off location sharing. The second thing I do is open the Face-Time app.

"Calling your dad?"

"Not him. My mom. I have to tell someone about this insane shit."

"I'll give you some space." She turns toward the tent, but I reach for her elbow to stop her.

"I want you to meet her. Through FaceTime, where your life isn't in danger because of the psycho men in my family."

"Are you sure?"

"She needs to understand you're not the bad guy in this situation. And if she sees what Teague did to me, she will."

"Alright."

The line only rings once before my mom picks up; Dad must not be around. "Hi Jul—what in Christ's name happened to your face?"

"Teague."

"Excuse me?" Her voice drops half an octave.

I don't know what to say, how to phrase it. There are no words on the tip of my tongue; I'm drawing from an empty well. It was unfathomable. It shouldn't be; I know Teague's temperament. Still, we've been so close our entire lives. He truly is the nearest thing I have to a brother. I feel that way about him in my heart; it wasn't a line I fed him to get my way. And because we love each other I never thought he'd hurt me. Turns out his love comes with terms and conditions.

Rowan sees how much I'm struggling, mouths *I've got this*, and pops into the frame. "Mrs. Calloway, your nephew showed up to where we're staying. He tracked Juliet's phone. When he found us together, he got aggressive. He drew his gun. We fought. Jules tried to stop him, and he hit her with it. On purpose. I reacted very poorly to that because I love your daughter. I couldn't stand to see her hurt and I was worried that he would... do something to her that *wouldn't* heal. Teague is on his way to the hospital. He'll be fine, but it's gonna take a while. I'm so sorry I couldn't keep Jules from getting injured, and I'm sorry that I let my anger get the best of me and hurt Teague so badly. I'm not a violent person, but I do a violent job."

My mother's lips are squeezed in a thin, tight line. *That's not anger, it's rage.* The question is, over what?

"My nephew struck my daughter with his gun." *Oh.* It's not in any way an interrogation. She's sorting through the facts.

"Yes, he did."

"And you gave the little shit the whooping he should have gotten ages ago from his father."

Rowan is so taken aback her eyebrows look like they're climbing up her face to hide in her hair. She clears her throat. "Yes, ma'am, I did do that. Yes."

"And you love my *topolina*."

"Mom!" *Never too old for your mom to embarrass you.*

Rowan glances at me, confused.

I mumble, "It means little mouse."

Rowan's grin lets me know she thinks it's endearing. "Yes, I do. Very much."

"Well then. Thank you for taking care of Juliet even though it meant putting yourself at risk, and making some hard choices."

"I'd do it again. Although I'd prefer not to have to."

"Yes, I think we would all prefer that."

"Definitely," I chime in.

"This is only going to escalate. We may need to come up with an exit strategy for you both." There's a sly glint in my mother's eyes as she says it, like she'd been plotting this course for a long time.

"An exit strategy." Rowan mulls. To me, she says, "You take after your mom a lot."

"I like you," my mom tells her.

"Honestly? Same, Mrs. Calloway. None of this was something I chose. I was born into it, and my dad is—"

"I understand. I do." Mom frowns. "Give me some time to think, girls."

"Rowan had an idea. A good one. Although, it might be extremely hard and expensive to pull off."

"Let's not discuss it on the phone. Was Teague conscious on his way to the hospital?"

I nod. "Yes, but not in any shape to talk."

"I hate to say it, but that's beneficial. If he can't talk about what happened, it'll give us time."

"Should I come home?"

"No. Gino's wake is tomorrow. His parents are burying him Saturday."

Oh, no. Teague is going to miss it. That's something I do feel bad about. Rowan sighs, rueful. "I want—" she starts, stops, considers. "It's not enough, nothing I can do would be enough, but I want to send a funeral spray. Anonymously. Is that crass? I... I don't know." Her voice trembles and her eyes are glassy, shining with a hint of tears.

"It's a lovely thought, dear," my mother says. "I'll text Jules the funeral home details."

"Thank you."

"You should leave wherever you are. Teague might have told someone where he was going."

"I thought that, too," I add.

Rowan agrees. "For sure."

"I'll let you know when we've heard about Teague through official channels. Until then, stay hidden."

"We will. Thanks, Mom."

She hangs up. A few seconds later a text notification pings. It's the address to O'Keefe's Funeral Home in Cambridge. Rowan nods and nods, then goes to retrieve her phone from her bag. I'd asked her to leave it this morning so we could be together without distraction. *Hilarious, karma.*

She returns and collapses into the second chair, opens a browser, and finds a local florist. "I've sent a few funeral arrangements before, but those were always easy. Not personal, just whatever ornate thing popped up in the search and looked expensive. I can't do that this time."

"We can choose one together."

She scooches her chair closer to mine and starts scrolling through the options—bouquets in vases, casket covers, standing arrays. We decide on the latter. "There's a build-your-own option. Did he have a favorite color?"

I smile at the memory of Gino in middle school, explaining to Teague and me why he loved autumn; the trees turned his favorite color. "Orange."

"Asiatic lilies, orange roses, and white chrysanthemums," she says. "That'll be perfect."

I'm not shocked that she knows about flowers. She knows a lot about a lot, especially things she likes. She likes sharks and fast cars and books and flowers. Hard and soft. Balanced.

SIXTEEN

ROWAN

We change out of our battle-worn clothes before we leave. I'm in black jeans and a black t-shirt—it's not a matter of noticeable bloodstains, but I feel the sticky fluid congealing in the fabric, and I hate it. The sweater I gave her to wear on the boat is white, and it's fucked. Her blood seeped into the collar and the sleeves when she wiped at her wound, and I hate it twice over. I'd burn it in the firepit if I weren't so abysmal at lighting the goddamn thing.

Jules decides she wants to break down the tent and take it with us. She's sweet and sentimental and, as much of a cluster-fuck our "first date" has been, it's a memento. A trophy to remind us that the odds are stacked against us, and we're in the messiest ever mess, but we're going to win by sheer determination alone. I plead my case that we might not have time: Her father's henchmen could be on their way to us as we speak, it's only a possession, and we don't need it. She flashes me *those* eyes. I know she's trying to manipulate me, but recognizing that and giving in anyway doesn't make me a sucker, it makes me kind. "If it's that important to you, fine." I get to work. She tries to help but only ends up getting irritated. I ask her to take care of the air mattress instead.

I'm not "butch" per se, but it's becoming clear that I'm better at the "boyfriend jobs." Gender roles are trash, and I don't believe they should exist, but it's good to know our dynamic. Like, I know she cooks and she's good at it. Her mom taught her how. I don't fucking cook unless I'm aiming to assassinate someone discreetly without the need for poison. She knows I enjoy doing laundry. The simplicity and repetitiveness of it relaxes me. She loves clothes, abhors laundry. Dynamic.

I manage to get the tent folded small enough to fit in its travel bag and we're out.

The car situation. Do I take the whip I stole? Dumb idea. A stolen car will end up drawing attention to us. The cars I've stolen in the past were luxury brands for international buyers in Russia or Qatar, or wherever the fuck my father sends hot merchandise.

The Camaro is coming up fast. I gotta tell her. "Um, I wasn't bullshitting when I told you I had a problem with my Jeep. What I didn't tell you, and what makes sense now, is that I had to ditch it because your cousin had me in a high-speed chase on the I-95. I didn't know it was his car; I'd never seen it before. All I knew was someone was following me."

"Rowan," she groans, "this is the kind of knowledge you have to drop on me. I get why you didn't; you thought it would scare me. Please don't try to be my father and shield me from everything, okay? We're in this together, and little spills are easier to clean up than big ones."

"True." It's terrifying how rational she is. She'll never have to try to manipulate me; all she'd have to do is logic me. Emotions are arguable, cool-minded calculations; facts are not.

She pops the trunk of her white Beamer and I shove the tent and my duffle into it, followed by her luggage. Then she's cracking up, unprompted, like a madwoman. All I can do is gawp at her as if she belongs in an old-school asylum for the insane. "That." She points at the Camaro parked a few spaces behind her. "That's the car you stole, isn't it?"

"Yeah."

"It's hideous." She covers her injured brow to keep it in check as she laughs harder.

I can't not laugh. She's right. "I didn't have the luxury of searching for an aesthetically pleasing vehicle to boost, Juliet."

"I'm glad we're leaving it here." She hands me her keys. "I don't know where we're going, but you drive."

I pitch the suggestion of going to Canada. I'm following the maps app to nowhere and we're heading north anyway. We can be over the border in three hours. Jules humors me with ideas of what we could do in Montreal—botanical gardens, art museums, shopping on Rue Sainte-Catherine. She's traveled more than I have and has been there before. "I bought my favorite pair of Michael Kors boots there." Eventually she wakes herself from the beautiful daydream and brings us back to earth. "I don't have my passport with me, though."

Damn it. I have mine. My villainous mind starts contemplating ways we could cross the border illegally. I'd drive through a cornfield if I had to. I don't think Jules would be thrilled about it. "It's wild what a law-abiding citizen you are, considering you're mob royalty."

She gives me an eyeroll. "Oh, please. You like good girls. Elisa's more of a good girl than I am."

"Of all the women who have actually been with me, you're still on the one who hasn't?"

She flips her long blonde hair at me and sulks. "Yes. I don't care about the women before me. She's, like, concurrent with me."

It's been a rough day in every sense of the word. She's tired and ornery. "Okay, but I'm not tryna flee the country with *her*, am I?"

I shift my eyes from the road and catch her squinting at me, bothered that I shut her down with a lone sentence. "You couldn't just let me be mad for no reason for *five* minutes?"

"No. That's a girl game I don't play."

She leans over the center console, stretching her seatbelt to its limit to kiss me. "I love that about you. You won't let me get away with throwing a fit."

"You're not an unreasonable spoiled brat so why bother pretending to be?"

"Because it's fun to wind people up sometimes."

I don't see the appeal. Winding someone up in my line of work? Someone would end up with their teeth bashed in. "Whatever you say."

There's a sign on the side of the dusty country highway that reads *Chandler House Inn, Two Miles*. A random inn in a nameless Maine town is as good a place as any for two runaways to get some respite from the day's craziness. It's starting to get dark, and I'm aching from head to toe.

"Google that joint." I motion to the sign.

She does. "It's a five-room bed and breakfast in a converted Victorian mansion. There's a swimming pool, and the two suites on the ground floor each have a private jacuzzi. Ooh. That would be a very good thing for your muscles, which I'm sure are killing you." No joke. She's been watching me try to loosen myself up for an hour.

The beating I doled Teague was not my first rodeo. And Jules is too intelligent not to know that an ice bath would be better. I see what she's doing. She's had to be wily her entire life in order to gain any freedom or an identity of her own. Sooner or later, it'll sink in for her that she doesn't have to be that person with me. "Just say you want a tubby, Jules."

"I want a fucking tubby."

"Okay, my love. You shall have one."

Driving though Gray, Maine, it irks me how eerily quiet it is. Not that I expected a bustling nightlife from a tiny, one-tavern town. But it doesn't have a quaint seaside village vibe, more like something from a horrifying zombie video game. The fog rolling in, smokey and iridescent under the streetlights, is not helping the atmosphere.

Chandler House sits atop a hill. Its driveway is unpaved. The BMW churns up gravel and pebbles the whole way. There's a parking area with only one space taken. I occupy the one beside it.

"I can't decide if this feels cozy or if we're about to walk into a remake of *Psycho*," Jules says as we're ascending the wide verandah to the front door. *Psycho* I could handle. It's "cozy" that makes me anxious. I thrive in chaos. It's been my default state of being for twenty-three years.

We enter the inn. Jules goes straight for the antique wooden desk with a handwritten sign that reads *Check In* and rings a small gold bell. The ting reverberates for a while. When no one greets us after a minute, she rings it twice more. *I feel that.* It's not out of character for her to be impatient, but it is for me. I understand where it's coming from. I want to get into a room, a closed space that's unlikely to be intruded on, but that I could defend if it were.

A woman with salt and pepper hair comes jostling down the winding carpeted staircase, appearing disheveled as she ties her bathrobe closed. "Hi, hi, hello!" she singsongs. "So sorry, wasn't expecting any guests tonight."

Jules beams and turns up the charm to eleven. "Please, don't be sorry. We're sorry not to have made a reservation. We were just passing through town, saw this beautiful inn, and felt so drawn to it! It seemed like a very comfy place to get some R&R

for a few days." She gestures to her forehead. "Surfing accident. Do you have any rooms available?"

The woman is downright enchanted. Hell, I am, too, even though I know Jules is bullshitting and have been able to see through her glossy veneer from day one.

"We do! I have one on the third floor, very spacious, and the Grand Suite on the first floor. That room has a hot tub."

"That sounds lovely. What do you think, sweetheart?" She makes a show of consulting me.

I fight the urge to shoot her an eyeroll and nod instead.

"We'll take the suite."

"Wonderful. And that room is open until Monday. How long will you be staying?"

"Let's book it through Monday."

"Great. I'll just need a credit card to have on file."

Jules falters ever-so-slightly. It's more than the fact that her dad controls her finances; credit cards are trackable—either of us using one could mean trouble. Right. Money is the solution to almost every problem. If money can't fix it, it's not a problem, it's a crisis.

"How about I pay cash up front," I wager, "and put down a nonrefundable cleaning deposit on top of the room fees?"

Jules winks at me. Her posture reverts to easy breezy. "We try to live within our means."

The woman examines us. Per usual, Jules looks well put together and stylish in her Calvin Klein V-neck dress. *Glad I changed into my daily standard business casual.*

"Unorthodox but, sure."

She gives me a price. I offer an extra hundred bucks a night. She agrees. I sign the old-fashioned guest book with my dead mother's maiden name and the address for the John F. Kennedy Library. We make the exchange—cash for a room key. "Your room is at the back of the house, down this corridor here, off to the right. Breakfast is served at eight thirty."

Jules thanks her. All I can muster is a polite grin as my inner voice berates me: *Why you gotta make everything so seedy? It's not normal.* No, it's not. I long for normal. Maybe someday.

Jules is right that the searing water relieves my tender muscles. I'm aware heat exacerbates inflammation, but I don't give a shit. I want instant relief. I get a FaceTime call as Jules is about to submerge her naked body in the hot tub. It's Merrick. I answer with audio only. He doesn't question it or greet me with any civilities. He goes straight to it.

"Bro, what the fuck did you do?"

What haven't I done in the last few days? "Guess you heard."

"That you shot one of Calloway's guys at the marina, he bit it, and now you're on the run? Yeah, I heard. Why'd I hear it from Ben and not you?"

"I haven't had a lot of time to chat, Mer."

"Oh, and Ben's out and going to Estonia or somewhere in Europe with his dad?"

"Europe is news to me, too. But yes, I got him out."

"Why?"

"You know why."

"Was it him or Alistair?"

He knows damn well it wasn't Ben. Ben's my guy, not my father's. I don't strongarm my guys into submission, or put the fear of God into them. I wouldn't give anyone a reason to turn on me; it's better to be respected out of love than respected out of fear. That's how you earn and keep loyalty. It's a concept Callum Monaghan never grasped.

"Alistair."

"Is there anything else?"

I tell him I ruined the most perfect day of my existence by

almost thrashing Teague to death on a scenic beach while his cousin, the woman I love, watched.

He heaves a sigh from deep in his chest. "I'm never going to see you again, am I?"

Hearing him say it, the hopelessness of his tenor, makes me consider lying, but he'd be able to tell. "I don't know."

"Take me off speaker."

Shit... "Okay, done." I bring the phone to my ear.

"Is she worth it?" he murmurs. "Everything you've had to do since you met her. Everything you're giving up for her."

Tension between our families has been building for years. I would have had to defend myself against the Calloways in due course, once things became untenable. Falling in love with Jules sped up the arrival of an inevitable outcome, that's all.

"Yes. But losing you and Ben, that's the one thing that hurts. I haven't said it enough, or maybe I've never said it at all, but I hope you know that I've always loved you both and I always will."

He gets choked up and doesn't try to cover it. "We love you, too, you idiot. If there's anything I can do—"

"I've kept you in the dugout as much as possible for a reason. Don't try to make it to the starting lineup. Stay as far away from this disaster as you can."

"I will. As long you know I've got your back should you need me."

"I do know that. You're my main dude. I appreciate you."

"Take care of yourself, Row," he says and hangs up.

Jules slinks across the hot tub to sit next to me.

I put my arm around her shoulder and hold her close. "Have you talked to Rose or Shannon?"

"No."

"You should get on that. If Merrick was worried, they will be, too."

"We're terrible friends, aren't we? Terrible friends, terrible daughters. I'm a terrible cousin."

"Maybe. But a lot of that is what we were made to be. We can try to be better at one of those things. We choose our friends, and they choose us."

"You've got some Yoda pearls of wisdom."

"Try, I do, young Padawan."

"I'll call them tomorrow."

"Good."

She snuggles into my shoulder. I play with the wisps of hair coming loose from her messy bun. "I'm drained," she says through a yawn.

"Same."

"Hey, you know what? Tonight will be the first night we sleep together without having sex."

"That actually sounds nice, but, uh, let's not make a habit of it. Cool?"

She laughs against my skin, then looks up at me and goes, "That's the most fuckboy thing you've ever said to me."

That's because I'm not one with her. I couldn't be if I'd tried. Sex is important, and ours is fire, but I've been all in on her from the start.

SEVENTEEN

JULES

Rose is crying. I catch her right after she gets home from Gino's wake. They weren't besties or anything, but they were definitely friends. And she's delicate, unused to violence and loss. Outside of her dog getting hit by a car when we were twelve, she's never really lost anyone or anything she loves. Both sets of her grandparents are still with us. She's had a sheltered life. Her parents are teachers; her older sister is a teacher. She's going to be a teacher. What a thing to have run in your family: The calmness of the American status quo. I envy her. I think that's the main reason why I bothered with college. I didn't have to go. I won't have to work after graduation if I don't want to. My dad's wealth is dirty but well-hidden, and I could siphon off of him until he dies, then when he goes it'll be mine. But going to college was a choice I was allowed to make, and it gave me a semblance of normalcy I never had.

"How can you not be furious at Rowan? I'm mad at her," Rose wonders.

As much as I've tried to deny it, part of me is somewhat angry with her. I hear its foul hissing in the recesses of my brain. But it's very quiet, drowned out by my anger over our circumstances, over the choices that we weren't given, over the total lack of control we've had over our own lives up to this point. Kill or be killed is for ancient times, when the Neanderthals had to slaughter saber-toothed tigers to avoid becoming their lunch. That way of living is unnecessary now. Some men missed the memo.

"I can't explain it to you. You wouldn't understand."

"Like how you didn't *understand* when I told you getting with Rowan was a bad idea?"

"I understood. I ignored you." Her allure was too intense not to.

"Yes, you did. Whatever... Your parents were at the funeral home, but I didn't see Teague."

He's hanging on by a thread in a hospital bed. "He's indisposed."

"What does that mean?"

It's a good thing she doesn't know. It means no one besides my mom does. I don't want to tell Rose; I don't want her involved. And I don't want her to hate Rowan. She's already tiptoeing at the threshold.

"He went out of town for a while."

"Fine, we'll go with that." She lets it drop. "Speaking of out of town, when are you coming home?"

"I haven't figured that out yet."

"I'm glad you're alright. Took you long enough to call."

"I know. I'm sorry."

"The flowers Rowan sent were nice."

"What?" I know she didn't sign the sympathy card. I was right there beside her as she ordered them.

"Don't worry, nobody but your mom and I figured it out."

"How?"

She sniffles. "Your mom knows we talk about everything. She told me she spoke to you and Rowan on the phone and that Rowan wanted to send flowers. They were the only orange ones, and they had no sender info. It had *you* written all over it. Tell Rowan hers was the most impressive arrangement there and Gino's parents thought they were beautiful. His mom said, 'Whoever sent these must have really cared about G.'"

I'm crying all over again. It's a wound that's not going to heal, only become more bearable with time. The hiss of anger at Rowan is a little louder in this moment. I can distinguish it from the rest of my resentment. My girlfriend shot my friend and he's gone. No more fall foliage for him.

I glance across the suite at Rowan, lounging on the bed, reading *The Book of Unusual Knowledge*. She grabbed it from her bag so she'd stop obsessively checking the time on the bedside clock. She knows the funeral reception hours are between ten and two. She did care about Gino—didn't know him from Adam, couldn't have even told you his name—but she valued his personhood, his life, nonetheless. And she'll hate herself for the rest of hers for taking his. She is not her father. I love her *because* she is not her father. I wipe the tears from my cheeks. "I'll let her know. Thanks. Are you going to the cemetery tomorrow?"

"No. It's too much for me."

"I get it. The finale." It's a lot.

"Right."

We say our goodbyes and hang up. I join Rowan on the bed. We've established a routine that I'm loving: I rest my temple on her shoulder, she automatically slings her arm around me, coaxes me closer to her and rubs my skin with her thumb. Amazing how quickly couple-y habits develop between two people who are right for each other.

"Gino's parents appreciated your flowers," I mumble into her clavicle.

She closes the book. "I'm glad. But it's not sitting right with me that you and Teague are both gonna miss your chance to say goodbye to your friend. And it doesn't feel right not to pay my respects, either."

"We can't go." *She can't go.*

"Juliet Calloway, we can do anything. It would be stupid for Rowan Monaghan to show her face there, but... that incognito idea I had for your graduation? Let's test it."

My heart drops. Thus far, loving her has been an introduction to anxiety, which is how I know it's real. "That cemetery will be the least 'safe space' on the planet for you. All of my dad's henchmen will be there."

"I'm aware."

"You talk to me about how surprising my morals are when yours are even more so."

"I'm responsible for this funeral, Jules. It's not morality, it's penance."

I cannot dispute that. If I tried to, I would lose. There's nothing to do but capitulate. And I would very much like to go. "We can't show up together. There's going to be too much attention on me and my family."

"I already figured that."

"Get up." I roll off the mattress.

She places the book on the bedside table. "Why?"

"We're going shopping so you can play dress up."

"I don't think I've played dress up before. Probably gonna be shitty at it."

That's no shocker. "There's a first time for everything. And no worries, I'll teach you what you need to know."

———

Shopping with Rowan is not the fun movie montage that shopping with Rose and Shannon is. She's the type of person who goes into a store with a singular focus, purchases the items she needs, and leaves as quickly as possible. And she doesn't like crowds. Crowds conceal threats. It's raining, so the Maine Mall in Portland is extremely crowded. I don't let go of her hand as we stroll through it, partly because I'm embracing my role as emotional-support human, and partly because holding hands in a mall is the most fantastically ordinary thing we've ever done.

Bloomingdale's is her aesthetic. The more femme part of the women's section is not. She's uncomfortable in every dress she tries on—this is the third. And we've established that she can't manage heels. It's a problem. As much as I adore her high-end futch style, we need to go in the complete opposite direction to make the ruse work. "Okay, babe, we can do flats, but the dress is non-negotiable."

"Yeah." She's standing tall and stiff in a black asymmetrical Armani. "Maybe something more trench coaty."

Hmm. That might be it. "A belted sheath midi."

"I have no idea what that is, Juliet." She shrugs and screws up her features in confusion. It'd be cute if we weren't shopping for a funeral outfit.

"It's... more trench coaty!"

"Great. I'm taking this thing off. What is with these puffy ass sleeves, for real? It's tulle. It's *tulle* and it's itchy." She unzips and lets the dress fall to the floor.

"That's a six-hundred-dollar garment. Have some respect."

"Fuck it, it doesn't respect me. It's hideous and scratchy." She pinches it off the floor, doing her best interpretation of the bend and snap—which I'm willing to bet she knows nothing about—and places it back on its hanger.

"Should I put my clothes on and go on a hunt for a trench coat dress or what?" she asks.

"No. You don't know what you're looking for. Stay here, I'll go."

"Thank you. For going along with this. And for loving me, even though I'm a FEMA-certified disaster area."

To think she has to thank me for loving her, as if it's a

burden. "Don't thank me for loving you. It's not a chore, I'm happy to do it. And don't thank me for going along with this, either. Once we're done here, we're hitting up a wig shop."

"Red and curly or nothing." She gives me an eyebrow wiggle.

Curly auburn isn't in any way inconspicuous, but I'll let her think it's an option. "We'll see."

EIGHTEEN
ROWAN

We're awake before sunrise; we have a two-hour drive to Forest Hills Cemetery in Boston and the service starts at nine thirty. I'm killing time waiting for Jules to finish up her routine, staring at myself in the wall-mounted gold antique mirror, and not recognizing my own reflection. The black "trench coat dress," the long, pin-straight blonde wig, the oversized sixties Jackie Onassis sunglasses. I look like a taller, curvier version of Jules. I dig her style. On her. On me it's ludicrous.

She comes out of the bathroom. I catch her behind me in the mirror. She's dressed to the nines yet wolf whistles at me. It's half sardonic, half legit. I lift the shades off my eyes and shoot her a glare.

"I mean, you've got legs for *days*." She leers.

"This will be the first and last time you get to choose my outfit for me, so enjoy it while you can."

She titters. "Oh, I am enjoying it. Kinda jealous that dress won't fit me. I like it."

"You could've bought one in your size."

She approaches from behind and pulls me tight to her small frame. "I'm trying to train myself to rein in my spending. We might be poor soon if we go through with the whole pricey alter egos thing, remember?"

"I'm skeptical you have it in you."

"I'll have you know my favorite hoodie only cost me ninety dollars at J. Crew."

I turn around in her embrace and laugh. "You get that ninety bucks is steep for a sweatshirt, right?"

She goes *tsss* but says, "Okay, yes."

I lean in to kiss her. "We should head out."

She inhales, exhales, agrees with a headshake, then grabs her car keys and her clutch from the nightstand.

———

This wig, compounded by the thickness of my own hair and the fact that I run hot, has me boiling. I'm sweating despite the BMW's icy AC. Poor, Lilliputian Jules is suffering the reverse: She's cold even though she has the passenger side vents closed. A shiver runs through her, and I envision us arguing over the ambient air temperature of an apartment we don't have yet. It's a dispute I'm stoked to get into someday. She'll win because I'll allow her to. I'll sweat my ass off in rooms that are ninety degrees in the height of summer while she's happy as a pig in shit, and I'll be happy because she is. Once in a while, if I'm noticeably uncomfortable, she'll blast the central air at sixty because, stubborn as she is, she's caring and considerate. Small compromises like those are what happy relationships—platonic, romantic, and familial—are built on. Give and take. What a wild concept, made wilder that I had little experience with or comprehension of it until *her*.

"You're thinking hard over there. Are you okay?" She tries to keep her teeth from chattering as she asks.

"Yeah. You aren't, though." Luckily, I had the insight to throw my leather jacket in the backseat. One-handed, I reach behind her, grab it, and drape it over her shoulders like a blanket. She cozies into it. I read her eyes as easily as I could a library book—she is completely in love with me. *Good. Same.*

Boston's city limit is fast approaching. My chest gets tighter with every passing mile. It's like I'm Giles Corey demanding more weight. If only being crushed to death by slabs of stone were a viable trade for a sick conscience in this day and age. *Could shoot yourself in the head or jump off a bridge or drown yourself in the sea...* No. That's a coward's move. I'm owning my shit until my natural end. I'm strong enough to carry the onus.

The Roxbury neighborhood where the cemetery is located is a place I'm very familiar with. Once a month I meet up with a man called Dante who purchases copious amounts of drugs from my dad and pays for them with a dollar-store backpack stuffed with twenty-dollar bills. Nice guy. He gave me a Christmas card last year, which was hella weird but thoughtful. I'd rather be here for an exchange with him.

I pull the car over in a public lot—the maps app tells me it's three blocks from the cemetery. "This is my stop. I'll walk the rest of the way and meet you back here when it's done?"

"Sounds good."

I move to hop out and Jules catches my bicep. "This is going to suck for both of us in different ways, and I hate that I can't be standing next to you."

"I hate it, too. But we'll get through it. And then we'll go back to Maine and take the rest of our weekend together, maybe have some more depressing sex?"

She lets out a sharp laugh. "We're such lesbians."

"Uh huh. Processing trauma as foreplay. Typical lesbo behavior." I give her a peck on the cheek. "Alright, let's get this shitshow on the road."

She takes my place in the driver's seat, then continues the journey to Forest Hills alone. I watch the Beamer as it zooms down the street past brownstones and high rises until it's nothing but a white speck on the horizon.

The cemetery is sprawling. It would be out of place in Boston proper. The burial grounds sprinkled throughout the city are small plots of land that existed before the population exploded and men built paved roads and bridges and towering buildings. Those gardens of remains are historic, headstones dating all the way back to the 1600s. Forest Hills is full of the newly dead—twentieth century corpses or later.

The black iron gates show no signs of rust. The grounds are well-maintained, green grass manicured to perfection, rose bushes trimmed and tame. There are fresh bouquets of flowers laid at the foot of gravestones I walk past. This is a place people visit, not a relic. Unforgotten.

It's a trek to get to Gino. There's a line of Porsches, Mercedes—all the impressive German car brands rich people own—parked along the service road, which is how I know where to find him. *Follow the gangsters.*

The gathering around the newly dug grave is considerable. I guess because Gino was so young, and death came for him too soon. So many black suits and black dresses. An ocean of black. In China, white is the traditional color of mourning. I remember reading that somewhere. It doesn't feel appropriate. White is hopeful, a blank slate full of promise. Black is emptiness, and what's a lifeless body but an empty shell?

I stand at the very edge of the group, the last wolf in the pack. Nobody seems to take any notice of me, the tall fake blonde in the back and off to the side, strategically positioned to take in the full weight of everyone's mourning. I'm just another funeral-goer dressed like the Void.

Up at the front facing the throngs are a middle-aged man and woman with dark hair and sad eyes. Their haunted expressions let me know they're Gino's parents. Next to them is a young woman, a teenager, who shares their coloring and their sorrow. Gino was a big brother. Discovering that hits me hard. The bond I stole from that girl is irreplaceable.

I notice there are many standing sprays surrounding the dark-stained mahogany casket. The flowers I sent are the prettiest, but that doesn't make me feel better. Catching sight of Jules and her mom, Maria, standing beside Patrick Calloway makes me feel worse. Not sad, pissed. I put Gino in the ground, but Jules is right that it didn't have to go down like that. And she's probably right that Gino and I would've been friends in another life—she knows us both well enough to call it. I bite back the urge to give Patrick the very public *fuck you* he deserves. That's the Monaghan training rearing its ugly head. I have to unlearn everything I was taught.

An elderly priest in a black and gold chasuble moves to the head of the casket and clears his throat. It's very Irish Catholic, as I suspected it would be. "We're here today to pay tribute to and remember the life of Eugene 'Gino' Murphy—son, brother, friend, and a man of God. He was called home to heaven much earlier than any of us would have liked, but we are grateful for the time we had with him. He had such a profound effect on his family, his community, and his church throughout his short life—"

I tune him out; most of what he's saying feels like utter bullshit. A man of God doesn't live a life of crime. Gino may have had a good heart, but that is the life he lived. He robbed, sold drugs, he would have done violence were he commanded to, and I'm sure he followed orders of that nature once or twice. Why do we try to put a positive spin on people after they die, when we know what kind of shit they got up to while they were here? I'm not going to heaven. The metric ton of shit I got up to punched my ticket straight to hell. My dad's gonna be driving the fucking bus that takes me there, and Patrick

Calloway will meet us in the seventh circle. Juliet won't be there. She's unpolluted. I'm gonna make damn sure she stays that way.

Gino's mother is sobbing and that's more worthy of my attention than some clueless, pious old man's words, anyhow. I should go up to her and offer my shoulder to cry on or some pathetic measure of comfort. *Got some nerve even entertaining that idea.* His father is not crying, but only just holding it together. He keeps bowing his head, concentrating on the lawn rather than the coffin in an effort to stave off tears. The sister has her bottom lip trapped between her teeth, trying her best to appear composed for her parents' sake, as though her pain is somehow less significant than theirs.

Juliet's brimming but refusing to let herself break down. Her mother's severe and somber. Patrick has his hands folded, forearms resting on his thighs, as if in silent prayer. It's a show of genuine contrition but fuck him all the same.

There's a strange disquiet rising within me, a hot air balloon gradually inflating. I didn't think this through. Being unable to control my emotions is so new to me—letting myself go beyond acknowledging that I have feelings and legit feeling them.

I have to stop watching these people, taking in their suffering. I allow my attention to flutter away from the funeral. From my peripheral vision I see movement on the winding service road beyond the sea of headstones: An enormous black SUV approaching, unhurried. It joins the line of vehicles parked for Gino's service. Latecomers? That's tactless. They must not have a modicum of decorum.

The SUV empties, three men the wrong side of forty wearing dark suits and darker sunglasses. As they approach, I see that the man in pinstripes is smiling. No, beaming. Wide-mouthed. Deranged. Insane.

Dad.

My pulse quickens as I watch him and his cronies reach

beneath their suit coats and reveal their weapons of choice: A SIG Sauer, a Beretta and a Walther PPK.

It's a subconscious decision to shout, "Everybody get down!" milliseconds before my dad and his men start shooting. It's not my warning that sends everyone into a whirlwind, but the sound and the shockwave of those initial bullets. Someone is hit. I'm not sure who or where, but there's an explosion of blood, misty in the air like red rain.

Panic. The crowd of mourners transforms into a herd of terrified human cattle. Some of them start running, and those are the ones ripe for picking. My dad feeds on fear and chaos. He loves it.

Jules. I don't see her mother or father. Most of the crowd has disbanded, but she's frozen in place; the only movement around her is from the breeze blowing through her loose blonde hair. Motionless, she is the perfect target for one of my dad's minions. I haul ass to her, fighting against my instinct to drop to the ground and crawl. "Juliet!" I scream. It's louder than I thought a human voice was capable of being, more thunderous than the gun blasts.

She sees me but, in her horror, doesn't recognize me. I rip the sunglasses off my face and the wig from my head, throw them to the ground. *Rowan*, she mouths.

Shells are flying all around us, ricocheting off tombstones, tearing flesh from bone. People are screeching in agony. I don't have the luxury of gentleness. I tackle her. She lands on the soft, springy soil with viciousness. I manage to cradle the back of her skull in my hand and absorb the worst of the blow. I examine her body for injury, for blood, for anything abnormal, any blemish to her perfect, beautiful skin.

"Are you okay?" I ask. She has the collar of my dress in her tiny fists. Her face is pale, and her blue irises are being swallowed by dilated black pupils. "Juliet, are you hurt?"

"No. No, I'm okay."

"Thank God. Thank *God*." I cling to her so firmly that I can feel her frenzied heart beating against my ribcage as if it were my own.

We've fallen behind a granite obelisk. We're well-concealed. She's safe enough for the moment, but the gunfire is getting louder. They're closing in. *They'll find her.* Or maybe the Calloways have started shooting back. I don't know. I can't see. I don't give a fuck either way; all I care about is Jules. I have to get her out of this cemetery.

"Stay down."

She cleaves to my forearm. "Please, don't go. Don't leave me. You'll di—"

I palm her cheeks. "I won't, my love. I won't die. Not today. We're both getting out of here alive."

My words are not a salve. I have to pry myself from her grip.

I peek around the corner of the tall grave marker to take a gander at the horror show unfolding. One of my father's douchebags, William, is sprawled on the lawn twenty feet from my position. He's bleeding from two holes in his chest. *One down.* Not too far from his position, my dad and Jeremy—the other fuckface he brought with him—are taking cover behind a mausoleum, now and again peering out and shooting wildly at nothing in particular.

To my immediate left, Patrick Calloway is on his haunches, stooped behind a marble headstone, returning fire in the inter-mittent silence. His wife is beside him covering her ears, hands soaked in the blood of a man splayed on the lawn just beyond her. Shot after shot after shot rings out from Calloway's Glock. He has better aim than my dad, and I find myself hoping he clips him—just a graze, so he'll stop fancying himself King Shit of Fuck Mountain and realize he's not invincible.

Patrick's magazine empties and he ducks down again. He reaches into his pocket for a spare clip but finds none. It was fortunate that he even had his gun on him. There's an unspoken

rule in the underground that days like today are automatic
ceasefires. Funerals and memorial services are sacred; weapons
are not needed. Naturally, in my father's twisted brain, a young
man's funeral is the perfect place for an ambush, all his enemies
lined up to pick off. That's him, a true villain at heart.

Calloway glances over at Jules, crumpled in a ball on her
knees, palms pressed against a giant gravestone. And then he
clocks me. The fear on his face for his daughter's wellbeing
turns to rage as he registers who I am. If he had a single bullet
left, I'd catch it right between the eyes.

"She's fine!" I yell to him. "She's safe with me, Calloway, I
swear."

Maria tugs his jacket sleeve. He turns to her, and she nods.
It's enough for him given the situation. "I'll break your fucking
neck if anything happens to her," he bellows back at me.

That's fair. "I'll break it for you."

More shots are fired from my right side. A Calloway guy. *Is
this ever going to end?* When he runs empty, there's prolonged
silence. Dad and Jeremy are out of ammo, too. My father's voice
shatters the quiet. It ripples through the air, angry and accusing.
Also, because I know him, I recognize the slight hint of alarm:
He has never *not* known my whereabouts this long.

"Where's my fucking daughter, Calloway? You put a hit out
on her? I swear on every saint you know, if she's dead—"

I stand up and step out from my shelter, undisguised, in the
full light of day. I could be shot by one of Calloway's men if
they have a fresh clip handy, but it's a chance I have to take.
Juliet reaches for me, pawing at the hem of my dress. I break
away from her.

"Dad!" I holler across the cemetery, hands up to show I'm
unarmed. "Dad, it's Rowan!"

Jeremy's is the face I see pop around the corner of the crypt.
His eyes bulge. He says something to my father that I can't

make out. And then Callum Monaghan unveils himself, tall and lanky and as ferocious as he's ever been.

"What the fuck are you doing here, kid?"

"Come on, Dad. You know why I'm here."

A hand takes mine, entwines my fingers. Jules stands tall at my side. Her tears have caused her mascara to run. The thick black lines down her cheeks look like warpaint, heightened by the sheer determination on her face. It's out now—us. We are the children of combating fiefdoms, daughters of defiance. The whole of Boston will know before the sun goes down. A lot of people will have opinions. The Rossi merger is off the table. There may be consequences for that. But the promises made weren't made by me, so let them rain hell on Callum and watch me shrug about it.

My dad examines us. I read the disgust on his mien. It's the same guise Teague wore in the tent, and every time he'd set sights on me before then. Love means nothing to men like them. They'll never understand its value. All they value are dollars and cents.

He motions for me to come to him with his index and middle fingers. "Let's go."

There are police sirens ringing through the ether and fast approaching. This isn't the Back Bay or Government Center or even Downtown—in this neighborhood gunshots are always gunshots, never firecrackers or cars backfiring. He turned this hallowed ground into a battlefield. If I had the physical strength to detain him, I'd make him stay to catch justice for it. If I had my piece, I might gun him down. I get it now: One way or another my father has to die, and his kingdom has to crumble alongside his brittle bones.

"I'm not going anywhere with you."

I watch his ego deflate as he says, "Please."

Didn't think he had that word in his vocabulary. "No."

He flinches at the understanding that he has unequivocally and forever lost me.

I take in the aftermath of the shootout. At least six people caught a slug or two and are bleeding out in the grass. "William's dead or dying. I don't know who else is about to join him, but if you don't want to be dragged outta here in handcuffs, I suggest you leave. You don't have time to clean up your mess and you don't have the ammo to take care of all the witnesses."

"Call me when you come to your senses," he says, despite knowing that I already have. He turns back to the mausoleum and signals to Jeremy with a snap. Ever the dutiful soldier, Jeremy falls into step beside him. They saunter, nonchalant, to the SUV, then floor it out of the cemetery, leaving William by the wayside to rot like trash. A peon casualty. Predictable. He expects loyalty but has none to give.

Once the detritus from the SUV settles, the handfuls of mourners who scattered to the wind regroup. Some rush to help the fallen, others—the mobsters—rush to leave before the police arrive to ask questions.

Jules's hand is still in mine. Even as her parents approach us, she keeps holding on. I'm grateful Patrick Calloway can't shoot lasers from his eyes—neither Jules nor I would have hands left if he could.

"Of all the women in this city you went for the only one off-limits." I can't tell if he's talking to Jules or me. Maybe it's both. There's no question his follow-up is directed toward me. "You protected my daughter and for that I'll let you live. Go. Now. Back to wherever it is you've been hiding like a coward."

"Dad—"

"She killed one of my men and nearly killed your cousin." Jules and her mother both gasp in unison. Patrick nails Jules with a scowl. "You think I didn't know there was something going on between you? I figured it out the day she shot Gino, and you blamed your family for it instead of her. Teague's a blockhead and even he figured it out. I suspected you'd be with her, so I gave him permission to find you and exact his revenge on her. I got a call from the hospital this morning. He failed; that's his fault. He won't fail next time. So run, Monaghan."

This son of a bitch. He knowingly put Jules in danger. I can't unlearn how to hate him while he keeps earning my hatred. "Take a good look at your daughter's face. That gouge in her forehead isn't from me—Teague did that. Your family, not mine. Keep him away from Juliet or the next time I see him I'll deliver his fucking head to your doorstep."

His maw curls like he's about to snarl. And on that note, he's done with me. "Juliet, you're leaving with us this minute, or I'll kill her where she stands."

She's torn. The battle she's fighting in her mind is written all over her body, from her green, grass-stained knees to her big blue eyes.

The cop cars are in view now. We all have to leave. "Go with them. It's okay." I pull my hand away from her.

"It's not."

No, it's not. But I have to believe that it will be. I want to kiss her goodbye and reassure her that we'll figure it out. I don't dare, under her father's scrutiny. He quickly ushers Jules and his wife toward the line of cars. He allows Jules to get into her BMW. She starts down the road first and he and Maria follow in their Mercedes. They exit through the gate on the far side of the cemetery as two cop cars pull through the main entrance.

I don't run. I make the rounds checking on the wounded. Two men and two women, no kids, thank fuck. Gino's family is unscathed. As far as I can tell, the only person critically injured is William. I have no empathy for him. *Death at a funeral, how fitting.*

The police arrive and it turns out that I'm acquainted with two of them. Partners. They belong to my father. Officer Byrne, the younger of the two, makes a beeline for me. "You can't be here."

"But—"

"Walk away. I didn't fucking see you." And then he's off to the scene of the crime to "do his job."

It's like I couldn't confess my sins if I tried to. Nobody wants to listen. The perks and the curse of being the sovereign of corruption's heir.

I wander the city aimlessly for a few hours, processing. The first thing I need to do is get back to Maine. I left a hundred thousand dollars in the safe in our suite, and I don't have anywhere else to be, anyway. And all my clothes are there. I'm dying to get out of this fucking dress. There's a car rental place in South Boston, about half a mile up Tremont Street from where I'm currently shuffling my sorry self. That's my destination.

I'm waiting at a surface road T stop for the Green Line train to pass, so I can cross the damn street, when a blaring car horn catches my attention. *Someone's laying hard on that thing.* A two-toned silver-black Nissan Z keels to a halt at the curbside a few feet in front of me. I know that car. I've sat my ass in the passenger seat many times. I approach it and find its blackout windows rolled down. Peering inside, a flood of relief washes over me.

"You're the messiest bitch alive, Row," Merrick says from the driver's seat.

"You're telling me, bro."

"You look wicked hot in a dress though." He whistles.

"Shut the fuck up."

"Get in." Once I'm in the car, seatbelt securely fastened per his request, he gets back on the road. The inquisition begins at the first red light we encounter. "Why didn't you ask me to come get you?"

"I told you, I want you to stay out of it."

"I am staying out of it. I'm picking you up after the stupid shit happened."

"How'd you know I was in Boston? Or where to find me?"

"Um, hello? Rose, my cousin, is your girlfriend's best friend. And news travels fast. Literally, the shootout was on the *News at Noon*. I just cruised the main streets around Forest Hill hoping to find you."

"Goddamn it."

"Yeah. What are you gonna do?"

"I don't know, Mer. I really don't." Everything is in the worst state of chaotic upheaval that I've had to deal with, like, ever. My life is unrecognizable. The status quo was never calm, but there was routine—objectives to achieve and directives to get me there. I'm good at critical thinking when there's a clear goal to reach. All this uncertainty... I'm a rudderless ship at the mercy of a tempestuous current.

"Well, I'm in. Wherever you're going, I'm going."

"What about your job?"

"I'll call out with COVID. I work at a print shop in the twenty-first century; how busy do you think it gets?"

I don't know why I laugh so hard but it's exactly what I need. "Wanna spend a weekend in Maine?"

He scoffs. "Nope. Ticks. But okay."

As he heads for the Zakim bridge to Route 93, I think about how much I love him, and how lucky I am to have him as a best friend.

NINETEEN
JULES

House arrest is coming. I'm aware of that reality the second I step through the threshold into the foyer. Under no circumstances will I be allowed past the rose bushes at the end of the driveway until I leave for Washington. We live in a historic house on Joy Street that's so grand it rivals estates in the English countryside, but it's no better than an elegant penitentiary. *I wonder if Dad has an ankle monitor ready for me.*

"Your cousin is coming home tomorrow," is all my father says as he enters the house on my heels. He's fuming and exhausted. There are still blades of grass strewn about his suit, the green aggressively bright in contrast to the matte black material.

"Oh, good. Will you be allowing him to smack me around again?"

He's struck by that. It's twisting the knife of his failure as a father—his greatest fear is being unable to protect me—but it's the only trump card I have to play.

He takes me by the shoulders as if to comfort me, but it's cold and I have no use for it. "Of course not. We'll be reevaluating his position in this family and this business."

"Good. Because Rowan meant it. If Teague ever touches me again, she'll lay him in his grave."

His jaw clenches. It's an automated physical response: He can't stand the mention of her or the fact that she's taken better care of me than he has. "And I would let her."

Thanks for setting up my argument for me. "Then how can you be so opposed to me being with her? She loves me, Dad. So much that she's risked her life for me *twice*. You saw that with your own eyes today."

"I also saw her father show up to a funeral service and start shooting people! Callum Monaghan raised her in a house without a mother to keep her soft. She is all him, a hundred precent *his* daughter."

"She's not! That's what you don't get. Somehow, in spite of him, she's better than him! And better than you."

"That's enough, both of you!" My mother makes herself heard. She's ashen-faced from the morning's trauma. A screaming match between my father and me is the last thing she needs. In true Italian fashion she talks with her hands, gesturing at the front door, then all around the hallway. "The world outside that door is chaotic enough. I want peace in this house. I want peace within my family. If you cannot speak to each other like calm, rational adults, do not speak to each other at all." She starts for the stairs. "I'm going to clean myself up and then take to my bed. If I hear either of you raise your voice—"

"I'm sorry, Mom. You won't."

"Good. Juliet Amelia, we need to have a conversation later, too."

I hate it when she calls me by my full name. She only does that when I'm in trouble. "Okay." *You know where to find me, since Dad's going to hold me captive.*

My mother disappears upstairs. My father steps out of his dress shoes, kicks them toward the timber shoe rack, and loosens his tie as he ambles to the living room. He sinks into his favorite reclining chair. It's not often I see him defeated, but he's rubbing his forehead, his face, as if he's unsure what else to do with himself. He's been living this perilous life for thirty years. Has he finally grown tired of his own hellacious creation? What will be the last straw for him? Losing my mother? Losing me? After today he must know he's on the precipice of both.

I collapse onto the couch opposite him, focusing on the whooshing of water through pipes as my mother turns on the shower upstairs. I don't want to talk to him about Rowan, but I don't want my love for her to be marred by guilt anymore, either. It has been, at least a little bit, from the start—that very first kiss. How something could feel so wrong and so perfectly right all the same is still beyond me.

My exhalation is a gale-force wind. "You know this has nothing to do with you, right, Dad? I didn't choose the daughter of your enemy to spite or hurt you. Love just happens. It's uncontrollable. If anything, I tried to fight it. But I lost."

He straightens himself in his chair. "I understand that. Your grandparents wanted to send your mother to Italy when she told them she was with me."

"Really? I had no idea."

"Yeah. They owned a bakery in the Bronx, and had a simple, happy life. I was twenty-two and already had a rap sheet. They saw me for who I was before I saw it myself."

I knew my parents met in New York on what my dad calls "a business trip," and that my mother is estranged from her parents. I met them once when I was very young. They were kind to me. I remember my grandfather was the first person to call me *topolina* and my grandmother cried when she hugged me goodbye. All this time, I didn't comprehend why my mom had shut them out. It was part of the choice she had to make.

"So, you left together?"

"Yes. Over the years, Maria tried to reconnect. But they

stood firm in their opinion of me. They were right all along, but she's a very proud woman. I'm lucky to be loved by her."

He's got to be fucking kidding me. "Don't you get that you're doing the same thing they did? You're pushing me out of our family."

"This is different. Back then I was a low-level nobody. Rowan is not. I have good reason to worry about you. *You* saw that today with *your* own eyes. It's clear you see a side of her I can't, all the things about her that have earned her your love. And yes, she does love you, deeply, I witnessed it—but she isn't safe for you."

"I'm aware. Although, to be fair, being your daughter means I'm unsafe by default."

"Which is the main reason I let you go to school on the other side of the country. You're a very smart young woman; you've probably known that from the beginning."

"I have."

"The difference is you will always be my daughter. To put it in terms your big math brain is more comfortable with, your mother and I are constants. Rowan is the only part of this equation that is a variable."

That's where he's wrong. Genetically, on a cellular level, he is my father, and that is unalterable. But Rowan discovered a way—albeit pricey and impractical—to make his presence in my life a mutable variable. I'm leaning more and more toward wanting him to be. I played the ace up my sleeve too early. Or perhaps I didn't have one to begin with. I can try to reason with an unreasonable man, I can bat my lashes at him all I like, but he's going to dig his heels in.

"There's nothing I can say to change your mind, is there?" I ask. "You're really not going to let me be happy, are you?"

"I can't, sweetheart. I'm sorry. I have to do what I think is right for you, and that's keeping you away from her."

"And you're willing to... do whatever it takes?" I can't say it aloud. I don't have to.

His brow furrows. "If it comes to that, yes. You think I'm as bad as Callum Monaghan. You're right, I can be. But I understand now how much it would hurt you if she died, so please don't make me *make it* come to that. If you truly love her, let her go."

Unacceptable. I gave him a chance to be sensible and he blew it. This calculation needs recomputing with new parameters. Elimination method: Subtract a coefficient to nullify a variable. *If that's how it has to be, that's how it'll be.*

"I guess there's nothing left to discuss."

He shakes his head. "No, there isn't."

"What about Callum and the Monaghan crew? You have reprisals in mind, I'm sure."

"Yes. He's going to pay for today."

He should. Although doling out justice isn't my father's job any more than it is Teague's or Callum's—that's what police are supposed to be for. But I don't have a care in the world about any of them anymore. Let them all kill each other.

I hear the shower in the upstairs bathroom go silent. Mom must be finished. It's the out I need to excuse myself from the conversation. I point to the ceiling, then at my chlorophyl-stained knees. "My turn to go get cleaned up."

"Good. Try to relax if you can."

Relax. Lol. "Sure."

"One more thing," he says to my back.

"Yes?"

"Give me your phone."

"I'm sorry, what?" My mouth falls agape out of reflex. Even when I was an actual teenager, he never took my phone away— because he could use it to keep tabs on me at all times. It's not an ankle monitor, though it may as well be. He doesn't need it to act as one while he has me sequestered. *What a power move.* I could pitch a tantrum like a petulant child. However, the man is tech incompetent and doesn't realize my iPad and iPhone share the same communication capabilities. I should play it up like I'm upset.

"This is a whole new level of tyrannical and it's not a good look for you. I hate it."

"I know you do, but—"

"It's for my own good, blah, blah, blah. Whatever. I'm not giving you the passcode."

"I don't need it." He's not interested in the content of my conversations, only in keeping me from responding to or initiating contact with Rowan. He's smart. I'm smarter.

"Fine." I turn the phone off, then toss it at him with more ferocity than I mean to. He fumbles and it hits the chair's armrest. He shakes his head but doesn't say anything more.

I think best in the shower. Maybe it's the heat loosening my muscles, or the absolute solitude that centers me. I appreciate the tranquility of nothing and no one requiring my attention or help, or of having to scheme, to avoid, or to twist someone to my will.

I scrub shampoo into my scalp, rinse it out, repeat the process with conditioner.

This is the part where I often imagine myself a droplet of water in the cascade. Unfeeling, unknowing, unaffected by manmade turmoil, with one singular purpose: To wash away dirt and stress. I envision soap suds dissolving as I make contact with them, then trickling down the drain enveloped by me. Of course, I end up in a sewer and the grossness of that visual always ruins my serenity. Funny how everything under the sun, living or inanimate, has the same cycle—clean to dirty, fresh to decaying, useful to useless. It's all connected.

Connected. A connected man is brought in for odd jobs and

vouched for by a made man, a recognized member of the organization. A made man reports to his captains, his captains report to their boss. My dad is their boss. That's the structure of the Irish mob, regardless of the family. Gino was connected. Teague is made, and a captain, though I don't know that he'll be a captain come tomorrow.

Made man. The phrasing is archaic. Not gender neutral, because historically women weren't included in the hierarchy, but Rowan's father only has one child, a daughter, and he molded her in his image because he recognized her talent and strength. She's made, and a captain. Alistair was also a captain under Monaghan... What is he to my father? Connected or made? Certainly not a captain, he's too green. But my father trusts him enough to have let him play both sides.

How any of this is useful information, I'm not sure. They're facts, not necessarily relevant to fixing the mess I'm in. It's a rare occasion that I struggle to find clarity; however, the hole I've dug is too deep to climb out of and I'm spiraling.

The truth is, buying myself a new identity isn't the answer to the dilemma. It could work for Rowan, but for me it's complex in a way that creates a different set of problems. Say I were to finish my degree. I couldn't use it. The credentials would be Juliet Calloway's, not Whoever Whatever's. I'd have the knowledge but not the hundred-thousand-dollar piece of parchment paper with my name on it as a testament to that. I'm not walking onto Wall Street or into an accounting firm without it. And if I can't work, I can't live. The point of getting an education was to get out from under my father's thumb and make my own way in the world.

We have to scrap that idea and start from scratch.

Right now, I don't even know where Rowan is, or what her immediate plans are. That's stressing me out above all else. I turn the chrome shower handle to the left and the waterfall above me transforms to dewdrops.

I forgo drying my hair or getting dressed in favor of quelling my anxiety; I need to see Rowan's face. I'm loosely wrapped in my fluffy pink bathrobe, sitting on my bed with my iPad in hand, EarPods in, waiting for her to answer my FaceTime call. On the fourth ring, she picks up.

I'm greeted by a backward baseball cap atop short, dirty-blonde hair, brown eyes, and chin stubble. "Hello, Juliet, nice robe."

I pull the robe tighter around my cleavage. "Merrick? What are you doing with Rowan's phone? Is she okay?"

He flips the camera toward Rowan, who's behind the steering wheel of what must be his car. She takes her eyes off the road for a second and locks them on me. "Chill, Jules. I'm fine. Everything's fine. Are *you* okay?"

"Physically, yes. Mentally, not really. I was in my first shootout this morning, my father wants revenge, and when we got home from the cemetery, he forbade me to see or speak to you ever again. He even went so far as to take my phone away."

She laughs. Fully laughs. It's the least expected and most inappropriate reaction to me expressing my agitation. "And yet, here you are, seeing and speaking to me. He can forbid you all he wants. We've got our hearts set on each other—he's fucked. At this point it's just a matter of how we deal with our fathers, that's all. Hell, let them hash it out and see who's left standing afterward, if it's either of them."

She hasn't seen me in a tailspin before, yet somehow manages to effortlessly pull me out of it. If there was ever any doubt that she's the one, it's squashed now. She knows how to handle me, while my own family doesn't.

"There's something else..." I tell her about my skepticism over becoming someone else, how it's even more impractical than a Calloway and a Monaghan falling for each other to begin with. She listens, patient yet intense. Strange how a person can be both of those things at the same time, but that's quintessential Rowan.

"Okay, so we scrap the idea. It was desperate and convoluted anyway. You've never broken a law and I've never been caught breaking one. Our names might carry guilt by association, but that's not a big deal. Maybe operating within the law, using it to our advantage, is the way to go."

"Something's cooking in that brilliant brain?"

"The first draft of something, yeah. But there are plot holes to fill in. We're on our way back to Chandler House. We're gonna call it home base for a while, I think. And I'll make sure to get your luggage and all your stuff back to you. Merrick can give it to Rose or something."

We're knee-deep in turmoil, yet she's still so thoughtful. "Thank you, you're sweet. And yeah, there are plot holes here, too. My mom has something she wants to talk to me about. I should get that out of the way."

"Good. We need to take stock of our assets and allies. Talk to her and get back to me, okay?"

"Okay. I'll call you tomorrow."

"Good. Bye. Love you."

"Bye. Love you, too."

Merrick clears his throat as if to remind us that he's there. Rowan goes, "Hang up the phone, you ass," and I giggle as he does. I have to admit I'm glad Rowan's not alone. Strong as she is, this is too much for anyone to shoulder on their own. I have my mom.

Suddenly, I'm curious how Rowan would have turned out if her mom had been around to raise her. My dad was correct about one thing: She'd probably be softer. The lack of balance affected her—no one taught her that softness isn't weakness. If she'd had a mother figure in her life, Callum wouldn't have been able to refine her steeliness without intervention. He's stone cold. It's sort of a miracle she maintained any kindness at all.

My mother planted that seed in me and watered it as best she could, violent surroundings be damned. It might have been Alistair's doing for Rowan. I don't know him well, but the few times he's come around he was courteous. Rowan said she learned manners from him rather than her father. If he nurtured the bright spot in her heart, I'm thankful for him.

I toss my iPad onto my desk, slide my earphones into their case, then shimmy into a pair of joggers and the only Gonzaga t-shirt I own. It's Saturday afternoon and I'm dressed like I'm ready for bed. I feel like I'm ready for bed, like I could sleep for days. That happens when I get anxious. My body isn't used to the influx of adrenalin and eventually needs to crash hard. I'm inclined to let it, once I've had my tête-à-tête with my mother.

I pad down the hallway to my parents' bedroom, noticing how cold the tile floor is against the soles of my bare feet. I hate being cold. I shouldn't be, summertime in Boston is hot as Hades, but my dad likes the damn central air set to the temperature of Snow Miser's lair, and gets pissed if I turn it up more than a degree. It's just another little thing about him that annoys me. Little things like that used to be easy to overlook; as I've gotten older, they've added up. I finally see the whole of him— he's the epitome of controlling.

I knock on the door. My mother answers, bedraggled. It's unlike her. She is the picture of composure. It's as if Italian women are preternaturally strong; there isn't anything that catches them by surprise or breaks their spirits. *Anything besides being shot at and/or watching people being shot.*

"Mom?"

She rests her temple against the doorframe and flashes me a smile. It's small and wounded, but all she can gather. "What a day, hmm?"

"Understatement of the century."

She leads me inside, closes and locks the door behind me. Locked doors are not allowed in this house. My dad flipped out once when I was in high school and accidentally hit the push-button lock on my bedroom door. He damn-near broke it down, banging on it like a zombie who smelled brains. I couldn't hear him because I had headphones on. He thought I had a boy in my room. He didn't even apologize once I'd opened the door and he realized I'd made a simple mistake and was alone. *"Never lock this door,"* is all he said. Since that day, I haven't. It makes uninterruptable privacy impossible. I never had any until I moved into my single room at school, but it quickly became my favorite thing about living so far away from my parents. *God, I miss being able to masturbate without worrying about getting caught.*

"Dad's not going to be thrilled about that." I gesture at the doorknob.

"Dad doesn't have a leg to stand on with me, at present."

Oof. Icy. I like it.

"I take it your father made his feelings about you and Rowan known."

"Loud and clear. He's not having it. I can't be around her or talk to her. If he had his way, he'd keep me from thinking about her."

"That's no surprise."

"No, but it's infuriating. Especially because he told me what happened between you and your parents."

"He thinks he has more power over you than they had over me."

"Doesn't he? The money. It all belongs to him. He pays for my education; I can't go back to school without him. And the reach of his influence... That's what scares me the most. What he knows and what he can find out and who will take his orders and who he can bribe. Imagine how much worse it would be if his operation was as prominent as Monaghan's? He'd be untouchable."

"The money isn't all his."

"What do you mean the money isn't all his?" It must be. My mother doesn't purchase groceries without running it past my dad first.

"Oh, *topolina*." She motions me toward the bed, taps the mattress. "Sit." She grabs her phone from her vanity, situates herself beside me, and unlocks it via Face ID. I watch her tap *info* and then toggle between the phone number everyone knows and one I don't recognize. What... the actual fuck? Who is this woman and what is she hiding? How did she hide it?

She clicks on a thumbnail of a sky-blue and yellow lion with the letters RIBB below it. Another screen pops open. It's a banking app. The Royal International Bank of the Bahamas. This app is advanced. She logs in using facial recognition. A few more taps and she's on another screen that reads *Allow Secondary Authorized User*.

She holds up the phone to me. "Look at the camera."

I'm so shocked that I look insane in the photo, eyes wide and mouth slack. A red warning flashes across the screen: *USER NOT AUTHORIZED*.

"Juliet Amelia Calloway, close your mouth and let's try it again."

My jaw snaps closed. The second picture grants me access to the account.

"One point six million dollars! Holy shit, Mom! You have an offshore account that Dad has no clue about?"

"Correct. I opened it a few days after I found out I was pregnant with you, and have been making weekly deposits ever since. Do you remember when I asked you a few years ago for a copy of your driver's license?"

I think back. It was right around my eighteenth birthday. "Yes. You said it was for a life insurance policy or something."

"It was. *This* is the insurance policy, in the event of the worst-case scenario. I was putting you on this account as a secondary user and needed a government ID to corroborate your birth certificate."

I feel like I swallowed a boulder. "Tell me you haven't been skimming from Dad all this time. He'll kill you if he finds out."

He could never forgive betrayal of that nature, irrespective of who the betrayer might be. He's too prideful and power hungry—examples must be made.

"Skimming," she scoffs. "He's so out of touch with reality, he's been handing me five thousand dollars a week for twenty-five years to run the house. I didn't need that much money. But he never asked for receipts, and I never offered any. After our bills were paid and the kitchen was stocked, whatever was left over went into this account."

"You're brilliant. And terrifying."

"I told you, you didn't get your brains from your father. Didn't I? I knew in the back of my mind this day or one like it would come. You don't need to worry about how to pay for school, or anything else for that matter."

I know what she means. "That isn't going to work out. The logistics of it... they don't exist for me. I know that I want my degree. I know that I want a career. Everything I've done up to this point, even my internship at Equity Financial, was done under my name. I can't give up Juliet Calloway, as much as I want to. And I *really* want to."

"So, we won't be arranging an elopement and faking your death, then?"

I give her an eyeroll. "This isn't *Romeo and Juliet*, Mother."

"I was kidding, sweetie." She pats my shoulder in the most sardonic way possible. "Give me your phone; I'll set up the app for you, so you can access the funds whenever you need to."

"Uh, that's going to be a problem. Dad confiscated it."

She sighs. "Of course he did." She flips through her phone wallet case, to a discreet compartment tucked behind the main cardholder slots, and pulls out a debit card. "Take this."

I examine it, turn it over in my hands. It's the strangest card, a black metal slate with no name or numbers stamped into it, one of those 'Tap to Pay' RFID icons in the bottom left corner, and a silver magnetic strip on the back. It makes sense that it would be unremarkable, given the large sum in the account, yet its inconspicuousness only serves to draw attention to its user. That's such a prototypical Rich Person Thing—ostentatious but sneaky, *"I'm a VIP, be aware of my presence but don't make a scene."* It hadn't occurred to me how crude that is until now. I've perpetuated it myself. Bougie is one thing, showy is another. I don't want to be that flashy girl anymore. A modest life is enough.

"Thank you. But this doesn't solve everything."

"How about we take away his money and influence? Let's burn down his stash house so he has to start from scratch."

"You got jokes today, huh, Mom?" I know my dad has a warehouse somewhere jam-packed with illegal goodies; however, I wouldn't know how to find it to burn it down. He guards its location with his life. He's smarter than Callum Monaghan in that way: Everyone knows where to find him, but few people dare to fuck with him.

"I'm only half joking about that."

"Do you actually know where the place is?"

She nods. "I do. My name was on the deed until I transferred ownership to him."

All these secrets I wasn't privy to. What else don't I know about my mom? "You transferred it to him? Why? Oh... Because you didn't want to be implicated in his crimes."

"Bingo." She reaches out to smooth my damp locks. "Once you came into the world, I couldn't afford to be involved with his business anymore. It was too dangerous. If anything should happen to him, I needed to be here for you. We both agreed on that."

"I could never do anything like that to him. I hate that he

deals in drugs and guns, but to be the one who robs him of his life's work feels wrong."

"Because you're loyal. And you love him."

Yes, and yes. "You, too."

"Indeed."

Knowing the whereabouts of his stash house could prove useful to Rowan, though. Whatever she's plotting, it's more nefariously ingenious than any plan I could hatch. Best to leave the masterminding up to her and take a supporting role. "Where is it?"

"On Constellation Wharf in Charlestown."

Charlestown. That's unexpected. When I think Charlestown, I think Bunker Hill Monument, retired naval warships converted to museums, a town rich with American history, not piles of cocaine and crates of handguns squirreled away in an Irish gangster's hidey-hole. It's a good location, right where the Mystic and Charles Rivers meet, easy to get to from the water. I'm filled with a perverse curiosity. I want to see it and all the merchandise it stores, gauge its size. Maybe then the true scope of my father's influence on this city will become clearer. I'm hoping he's more small-time than I've assumed.

"What's the address?" I ask.

"Sixty-five. The last building on the pier, closest to the water."

"And what's the security like? Cameras, an alarm system?"

"You know your father doesn't trust technology. He prefers good old-fashioned manpower. He has two men on guard duty at all times."

"Hmm." Two isn't bad. Men are dumb. I can manage two with a short skirt, a hair flip, and the Clueless Young Woman in Need of Assistance schtick.

"Why the piqued curiosity? You're not going to do anything foolish, are you?"

I most definitely am. I trust my mother implicitly. Still, if she can keep secrets under the guise of protecting me, I can do the same for her. "It's a lot to piece together, that's all. I'm having trouble digesting everything. I think it would help if I could see this place."

"That's reasonable."

"It doesn't matter anyway. It's not like Dad's going to let me go anywhere anytime soon."

"Not unsupervised." She's wearing a conniving expression I know well. She and I share it. How my father remains ignorant to it is unbelievable. "We are going shopping tomorrow. There must be a handful of things you need before going back to school."

Will my father buy that? We haven't done back-to-school shopping since freshman year, when they both flew across the country to help me move into the dorms, and then proceeded to buy me an entirely superfluous living room set. "I doubt Dad would let either of us out alone after today."

"He knows I can handle myself. And I always carry a snub nose revolver in my purse."

She WHAT? She's always despised guns as much as I do. My parents have had endless arguments about keeping any in their bedroom. The compromise was a biometric gun safe unlockable by either of them, and only them.

"Okay, I cannot handle any more revelations today." Actually, there is one more thing I must know. "Is it pink?"

"Absolutely not. It's Tiffany blue."

I don't know why I find that so hilarious, but I'm crowing. "Gives a whole new meaning to *Breakfast at Tiffany's*. I wonder how Audrey Hepburn would feel about it."

"Disapprovingly, I suspect."

"Okay. 'Shopping' tomorrow."

"Oh no, dear, we will be doing some shopping. We can't come home without a few big bags or Dad will be suspicious."

"Fair enough." And once I've staked out the warehouse, I'll

give Rowan a full report. Great. A plan is in motion. That's something. But without an endgame to focus on, I'm getting slammed with shockwaves from, um, being fucking shot at. I am not okay. How can I be? My mom and Rowan could have died this morning. I could have died this morning. The full weight of that is starting to sink in.

"Can I stay here with you for a bit? I don't want to be alone."

She paws at the corner of the duvet and folds it down. "In with you," she says like she used to when I was young, and she'd tuck me into bed at night. I stuff the debit card into my robe pocket and climb under the covers. She creases them tight around my body, then lies down next to me. She combs her fingers through my hair and starts singing, "*Ninna nanna, ninna oh, questo bimbo a chi lo do?*"

Memories surge to the forefront of my cognizance: Me at seven, spiking a fever, cranky as a hornet. Me at twelve, cut from the middle-school gymnastics team for being less coordinated than everyone else, and disappointed in myself. Me at sixteen, still closeted and heartbroken over a girl who broke up with me for a football player. This is how my mother calmed me every time.

I close my eyes and lose myself in her airy, ethereal voice.

I wake up alone. *Alone* alone—I scan the room; my mother is nowhere to be found. I check the time on the analog clock mounted on the wall across from the foot of the bed. It reads 8:15. The soft golden rays of sunlight peeking through the curtains momentarily confuse me. *Oh, 8:15 a.m.* It's Sunday morning. I slept for more than sixteen hours. I guess surviving the trauma of gun violence makes one sleepy. *Better than the alternative of not surviving it.* I wonder how many of my father's associates, or their innocent bystander family members, were casualties yesterday. Monaghan lost at least one man, I'm certain of it. I had a good view of him as we left the cemetery. Blood seeping from three holes—one in his sternum, two in his abdomen—zero movement, including signs of breathing.

My brain is foggy, zombified from too much rest. I need to chug a carafe of coffee in order to feel remotely human again. I check my robe pocket to ensure my "insurance policy" hasn't fallen out, then push myself up. My muscles scream at me and I don't know why they're as sore as they are. It has to be psychological, there's no other explanation. It's not like I ran a marathon. I didn't even have to run for my life. I was petrified, as in literally scared stiff. And I think Rowan knocked me to the ground? *Whatever.*

The hallway is quiet. I debate trudging to my room to throw on some clothes, but the way my feet are dragging that isn't going to happen. *Caffeinate first, function like a person later.*

I'm halfway down to the first floor when the front door opens. My dad enters and I hold to my steady descent but stop dead upon seeing Teague. His face is monstrous, purple-black and puffy. The left side is worse than the right. My dad told me he needed surgery to repair his broken cheekbone. I wasn't anticipating this result, however. It's as though there's a tiny, angry creature gestating inside the bruised, bulging bag under his eye. *Just a few more weeks 'til that baby's ready to pop out.* He's walking unsteadily, his gait favoring his right leg. Jesus, Rowan legit... Fucked. Him. Up.

I should say something to him. "You look like shit." *That was not the right "something."*

"I feel like shit." He groans.

Oh, poor baby. Have you chosen violence at every opportunity and those choices have finally caught up with you? "You earned it."

"I did."

Shocking admission. "Are you done now, or should I have let Rowan finish what she started?" I glance over at my father. He usually treats us like siblings, lets us hash out our issues without interfering. He's biting his tongue this time.

Teague shudders at the thought. "I'm done."

"Good." I point to my busted eyebrow. "Thanks for this, by the way." I can tell despite the ghastliness of his flesh that he's shamefaced. He should be. It's unprecedented that he raged out on someone he claims to care about.

"I'm sorry," he mutters, unable to make eye contact with me.

"Save it. 'Sorry' is for accidents. You meant to hurt me. And you would've done worse if Rowan hadn't stopped you."

"I—"

"Hello, Teague. Welcome home," my mother says from the space between the foyer and the dining room. Perfect timing. I didn't want to listen to the typical white-guy avoidance of accountability my cousin was about to feed me.

"Hi, Aunt M. Thanks."

"The three of you look like you could use a hearty breakfast. Everyone in the kitchen." And then she addresses my father pointedly. "Afterward, Juliet and I will be having some quality mother–daughter time at the Pru. Perhaps Newbury Street, too?"

"I do love Newbury Street." I give her a wink.

My father removes his phone from his pocket and stammers, "Alright, I'll send for Henry to accompany you."

"You will not. I said mother–daughter time and that is what I meant." The way my mom issues commandments is breathtaking to behold. She leaves no room for protest.

My dad doesn't try to make one. "I'd feel better if you'd let a bodyguard go with you, but understood."

"Very good. Come get some coffee, Jules, you look like death warmed up."

"Gee, thanks, Ma."

She throws her arm around my shoulder and escorts me into the kitchen.

Breakfast is awkward. Because of the silence, and also because Quasimodo sits across the table from me, mashing solid foods to paste so that he can masticate with minimal pain.

I'm all too glad to get the hell out of that house and away from the men. It's been so long since I've sat inside my mother's Maserati SUV that I forgot how simplistic it is in comparison to my BMW. There aren't enough buttons to press on the console. Rowan hates Maseratis. Lamborghinis and Ferraris, too. She calls them Italian trash. *"I want my clothes made by Italians and my cars engineered by Germans or get the fuck out."* My mom would not appreciate that. She swears by the superiority of Italian luxury across the board.

Any high-end vehicle in this part of Charlestown would stand out like a pink tutu at a Goth party. The closer to the wharf we get, the more dilapidated the buildings around us become. I know, intellectually, it's due to corrosion from the concentrated water vapor in the air, but that doesn't put me at ease. There's something creepy about manmade structures left to decay at Mother Nature's will. Maybe it's coming face to face with a force that's bigger and stronger than humanity, one that can't be reasoned with.

We approach a yellow road sign that reads *DEAD END.* No shit. From here it's a short drive off a long pier. My mother lurches the car onward until she reaches the faded outline of a parking space.

"It's that one." She gestures out my window to a building with peeling blue paint and a rusting metal roof. I'm not sure what I was expecting, but it wasn't this. It resembles a private jet hangar more than a storehouse. There are two enormous steel doors rather than a handful of smaller loading bays, with a line of squat windows on either side. To the right of the doors is a pop-up canopy, and a man in a folding chair seated beneath it. The second chair beside him is empty. *Two men on duty at all times. Where's the other one?*

A knock on my mother's window answers my question. "You can't be here," a man with a scruffy white beard says as Mom rolls down her window.

"Can't I really?"

"Mrs. Calloway!" The man gasps. "I'm sorry, I didn't recognize you. These eyes are getting old." Then his tune changes, gets leery. "I wasn't expecting you. Mr. C gives a holler if someone's coming down."

"We wanted to show our daughter what she'll be inheriting someday."

This is the exact right time to play the spoiled brat. I lean over my mother's lap. "You can go ahead and call my dad if you want to. I don't think he'll be very happy with your insubordination. You'll be lucky if all he does is fire you." For good measure, I flip my hair.

My mom plays along. "He's in a meeting at the moment. Surely, it won't be necessary to disturb him?"

The man is wide-eyed. "No, no, certainly not. You come on in, take a look around. Stay as long as you'd like."

Mom rolls up the window and grins at me. "Hell of a team we make." If gaslighting were a profession, we'd be the best in the business. It's not a wholesome skill to possess, but it's useful.

"Alright," she says, "let's go."

The building is like the Tardis, in that it's much larger on the inside than it seems from the outside. Coincidentally, it's the same color as the police box, but that's unimportant. What's important is the sheer number of wooden and metal crates lining the countless pallet racks. There must be hundreds.

"These can't all be drugs and handguns," I say.

"Would you like to find out?"

I would and I wouldn't. Once I've seen his wares, I become accountable for his crimes. As it stands, I have plausible deniability. But I need to know. That's who I am—curious to a fault. The saying goes "curiosity killed the cat," although that's not it in its entirety. The rest is "but satisfaction brought it back."

I spy a crowbar leaning against the wall a few feet from me.

"Yes, I would."

TWENTY

ROWAN

The morning sun is strong, but there's a cool breeze keeping the temperature down. We had breakfast al fresco, and now that he's done Merrick is throwing rocks into a pond that sits on the property behind Chandler House. They splash with a *plop*, sink to the bottom. I watch the sunfish and koi scatter.

"What're you doing? You're scaring the fish. And you could hurt them if you're not careful."

"Yeah, I suck at skipping stones."

"They have to be flat, and kind of potato shaped. Also, sidearm it like you're pitching a baseball." I find two rocks perfect for skimming water, pick them up, and toss one to him.

"You remember I'm a sidearm pitcher. How sweet."

"You impressed me with your strikeout numbers. I don't know why you didn't take that scholarship to Oregon."

"Because I didn't want to be a Duck."

"You're joking." I wind up, flick my wrist. My stone skips clear across the length of the oval pond, to the far bank and into long cattail reeds. It's been ages since I did this. Must be muscle memory. My mom loved it. She had a whole collection of puck-like pebbles. We'd go to the Frog Pond early Sunday mornings before Boston Common got too busy, skipping stones until I got bored and asked to leave.

"Duh. I didn't want to be that far away from my family."

"Interesting problem to have. Can't relate."

"I know." His second attempt is better than the last. The stone skips twice before it's swallowed by the water. "What're you gonna do about your dad?"

I grab a few more stones. He does, too.

"Can't kill him, I don't have it in me. There's no other way, I'm going to set him up for a fall." I tremble as I give it breath. It goes against everything my dad drilled into me about fealty and obedience. I've been the perfect drone.

Merrick turns the pebbles over in his hand. They clatter against each other. "Shit."

"Yep."

"Shouldn't be too hard though, right?"

"Nope." He has a cache the cops would have a field day sorting through. And I know all the cops on our payroll, so I know who *not* to call. The issue would be getting him to the boathouse where his hoard lives. He doesn't go down to the marina much unless he's taking one of his yachts out for a plea- sure cruise. He's been hands-off where merchandise is concerned for years; his captains deal with shipping, receiving, and domestic resale. Something big and catastrophic would have to go down in order to get him on site, but big and catastrophic could destroy the evidence before he gets there to take the fall for owning all of it. The only way anything will stick to the motherfucker is if he's caught with his grubby hands immersed in it. Then there'll be no denying or shirking ownership.

My phone rings in my jeans pocket. Someone not in my contacts is trying to FaceTime me. It's got to be Jules calling from her mom's phone. I hit *join* and smile at the sight of her. "Hey, beautiful."

"Hi." Something is off. She isn't smiling back at me. She's trying to hide that she's terrified. Her eyes give her away.

"Tell me what's wrong."

"I have good news and bad news. The good news is Teague is scared of you now so he's out of his vendetta phase. The bad news is my mom and I took trip to my dad's warehouse and... Well, see for yourself."

She flips the phone around. An open crate comes into focus, but I can't make sense of what I'm seeing: Small, green ovals that resemble turtle shells, with what looks like spray bottle nozzles sticking out of their tops.

Merrick gasps. "Are those fucking hand grenades?"

"Holy Mother of God, that's what they are?"

"Yes, that's what they are. He's got a warehouse full of them, maybe thirty crates, and large caliber guns, too. The kind soldiers use in combat." She pans the camera around the building. There are stacks and stacks of wooden crates with bits of straw packing filler sticking out through the slats. When she turns the camera back on herself, her eyes are welling with tears. "Where the hell did he get grenades, Rowan?"

From what I saw, they seemed old—leftovers from a skirmish that time forgot. There were white letters etched into the sides of them, but not letters I could read. They looked alien. Cyrillic? *The Cold War.* Fuck.

"Russia." The Russian mob has no presence in Boston. If they did, I'd know about it. They operate out of New York— Brighton Beach in Brooklyn. They're the craziest motherfuckers in the game, no morals, no ethics, shoot first ask questions *never.* Elisa's cousins in Manhattan had a problem with them not too long ago. Money couldn't satiate them; they wanted the debt paid in blood and they got it.

"If your father is in bed with the Russians, he's got a much broader reach than I realized." And he puts my dad's ventures to shame. My dad peddles drugs and guns to street thugs, and ships stolen Cadillacs to the Sultan of Wherever. Calloway is pushing weapons of mass murder in the Middle East or to warlords in Africa or some Godforsaken place.

I don't have to voice the concept to Jules; she's the smartest person I know and has already twigged it. "My dad's not a gangster, he's a terrorist. Hundreds, maybe thousands, of people are going to die because of him. I had no idea how dangerous he was. He can't be allowed to continue... *this.*"

She's correct. This changes everything. It's not about us anymore. Whether or not we can be together feels like a trivial concern when faced with the fact that Patrick is a fucking arms dealer a la the Merchant of Death. It doesn't make a difference whether his arsenal is utilized to kill Americans or Iraqis or Sudanese; we're all human beings. This is bigger than the Boston PD or State Troopers. It's FBI-level stuff, or Homeland Security, or some other national agency. *If he gets caught with weapons of war, he's looking at forever behind bars.*

Oh, shit, that's it! The one stone to kill two birds with. My father would die to get his mitts on Calloway's stash. And Calloway would die to protect it. "I have an idea. You're not gonna like it. I don't like it myself, but at this point it's not just for us, it's a public service. Neither of our fathers can be allowed to continue doing what they've been doing."

Jules looks at her mom, who's just off screen. I hear Maria say, "She's right. They've both become unmanageable. Enough is enough."

Jules swallows a lump in her throat. It goes down hard. "Are they going to survive this plan of yours?"

That is the goal, yes. But I don't want to make a promise I can't keep. If they choose to live that moment the way they've always chosen to live, they won't make it out alive. At least they'll have a choice. The consequences will fit their actions.

"I hope so," I answer. "That's really gonna depend on them."

"Not likely, then." She sighs. "How can I help?"

I didn't want her entangled in this, but it's unavoidable. I do need her help. We have to coordinate, or it won't work. "Merrick, take a walk."

"What? I want to—"

Maria pops on screen and uses her best Mom Voice. "You heard her, Merrick. Go on."

"Sorry, no boys allowed," Jules adds.

"Fine." He pouts, kicking up the rotting remnants of last autumn's fallen leaves as he trudges toward the tree line.

When I'm sure he's out of earshot, I start. "Alright. First step, I'm coming home."

———

An hour into the drive back to the city, Merrick breaks the uncomfortable quietness that has settled between us. "I could've lived without seeing your strap-on. How am I ever going to look at Jules the same way again? That thing is huge and she's so *small*. Where do you *put* it?"

"I guess I shouldn't tell you it vibrates then?"

Merrick goes bug-eyed. His cheeks are so red they're almost purple. "Good God, woman!"

"Hey, you insisted on helping me pack my bag. I told you to stay out of the zipped pocket, but you didn't listen."

"Maybe you should've told me why I needed to stay out of it."

"Right. Because 'Dude, my dick is in that pocket,' would have been less weird for you."

He shifts behind the steering wheel. "No. No it would not have."

"Exactly. Learn to listen to me when I say shit."

"Can we talk about something else? Like what your plan is."

"No. Don't ask me again." He doesn't listen to my words,

but he understands tone very well. He knows better than to push me when I get stern. He clears his throat as he straightens his backward baseball cap. His face tells me I've hurt his feelings. That isn't the desired effect.

"It's not that I don't trust you, man. I'd put my life in your hands, and I know my secrets are safe with you."

"I know. Thanks for saying it."

"Here's good." I make him stop the car at the top of my block. I don't want him any closer to my house or my dad than he needs to be. I tug my bag from the back seat. "If you can run Jules's suitcase to Rose, I'd appreciate it."

"No problem."

"I'm not sure how all this is gonna go, or how long it'll take to orchestrate. All I can say is I'm hoping that I get to stay after it's done." And maybe that the world will be safer with two treacherous men removed from it.

"Same." He wraps his arms around my shoulders, pulls me into a hug. "You're hella brave and hella smart. You've got this."

I don't wait for him to drive away. I have to move before my determination starts to waver. It's a 500-foot stroll to the brownstone that, a handful of days ago, every part of me was determined to never walk into again.

The march is automatic. My body functions without conscious thought. Before I realize it, I'm up the front porch, one hand on the brass filigree doorknob, the other sliding my key into the lock. The click it makes as it turns is strident—louder than a gunshot.

The house is still. Eerily so. It's not normally teeming with excitement, though there does tend to be a predictable flow of my dad's associates coming and going. He's showy, likes to entertain, likes to flaunt the promise of excess to his underlings, like, *"Work hard, kill a few people, and someday you too can have a two-million-dollar manse stocked with expensive liquors in crystal decanters."* There's nothing intrinsically wrong with wealth; it's the way he and Patrick Calloway went about attaining it that is all sorts of fucked up.

"Dad, are you home?" I check the living room and the kitchen, head up to his study. The door is closed, per usual. I give it the *shave and a haircut* knock. It's his signal that it's me on the other side of the door. He responds with *two bits* before opening. Or he used to. Not today. The door flies open sans ceremony.

"Well, well, well, if it isn't the pup running back to the leader of the pack with her tail between her legs."

You smug bastard. I ball my fists but stave off the impulse to lash out, or to turn around and saunter right the fuck back out of his miserable life.

"In case you were unaware, I took care of Teague Calloway. He's alive but won't be giving me any more shit."

He squinches and his glacial demeanor thaws. It was a test. He was goading me to see how I'd react, if I was in fact a scared puppy seeking the big bad wolf's protection. He understands now that is not the case. I am not here because I need him. I'm here because I choose to be. He welcomes me into his scared space, leads me to the familiar leather chair. Instead of sitting on the opposite side of the desk, he takes a seat beside me.

"I was sure I'd never see you again."

"I was pretty damn sure of that, too, after you fired a gun at the woman I love. You have Juliet to thank for me being here. She reminded me that you're the only parent I have left. You should more than thank her, you should kiss her ass in Macy's window."

He goes *hmm*. "She's a discerning girl."

"Don't mistake her sensitivity for forgiveness. She hates you for what you did at the funeral. I hate you for it, too. I don't care what happens to Calloway or Teague or any of their shitbirds, but if you ever try to hurt Jules or her mother again, I will ruin you. Do you understand me?"

He's not a man who takes threats lightly. Nor is he a man who shows fear. But I am the last person he ever imagined he would have to fear. "I do. You love this girl the way I loved your mother. I would've burned this city to the ground for her. But you know you can't be with her, right?"

Unaccustomed as I am to it, I have to lie and make it beyond convincing. "No, I can't be with her. You showed me how unrealistic it is to want a fairytale ending in real life. Don't expect a thank you."

"I accept that. But your lapse in loyalty needs rectifying. Are you willing to help me sort things out with the Rossis? Elisa was very hurt to hear that you were with someone else. Alfonso was none too pleased, either. He's a romantic. You know how Italians are."

"Yes. And if I do, can we forget all of this ever happened? I don't want to do menial tasks for you anymore. I want to see the books; I want to know about every single cent and all the inventory we have. I want to be ready for the reins when you hand them over to me."

He's surprised and a touch impressed. "Why the sudden change of heart?"

"I don't want your business, I'm just all you have. When it's mine, I'm going to run things very differently. I do like the money, and I'm going to clean it up."

"When it's yours, you can run it however you want." He grins. "We can move forward if you answer one question honestly. You warned Alistair I was coming for him, didn't you? He's gone off-grid. Ben, too."

I was waiting for that. I have a prepared response. "Did you think I wouldn't? There were times he was more of a father to me than you were. Remember all the back-to-school nights and basketball games you missed that he showed up for? I couldn't stop caring about him. You had my loyalty by default. He had it because he earned it, and because you encouraged it."

He folds his arms across his chest and taps his left bicep. "That is a fair point. He stepped in a lot when I couldn't be there."

Wow, an acknowledgment of weakness. "You're still hunting him though, aren't you?"

"I gave you the leniency you asked for with Ben because he never wronged me. Alistair has. Egregiously. I am who I am; don't ask me to be someone else."

There's the Callum Monaghan I know. "I wouldn't dream of it." Tigers can't change their stripes, but their teeth can be removed. "I have some information for you that I think will help me make amends for Alistair. But, before I give it to you, set up a meeting for me with Alfonso and Elisa. I want to take them to dinner."

"You mean you want *us* to take them to dinner?" He regards me with blatant concern—though for what, my wellbeing or his, I'm unsure—mixed with a hint of incredulity. He's not obtuse. He wouldn't have amassed his empire if he didn't dwell in a state of perpetual suspicion. I can't say I blame him for being wary of me. Anyway, he's right. I am going to pull a Brutus and stab him in the back. He's lucky I don't stab him through the heart.

Sell the shit out of it or you're screwed. "No, I meant what I said. It goes back to wanting to be an adult and, yeah, wanting to distance myself from you. You told me people fuck up under pressure and I'm no exception, but every time I've made a mistake, you've fixed it for me. *You* got the bullet from my gun out of Gino. *You* erased any traces of me from his body. I fucked things up with the Rossis. I hurt Elisa. This is my mess; let me clean it up. Otherwise, I'll never be able to own this city or do with it as I please."

He's glaring into my eyes, searching for any sign of deceit.

I'm praying to a God I don't believe in that he either can't see it, or he refuses to, because I know it's there. I'm the bearer of the heaviness, and maybe it's a lie too cumbersome for me to camouflage.

"I'll set it up for tomorrow night," he finally says. "You'll have to go to the North End. They'll want you off your game in their territory."

I mask my relief with an indifferent shrug. "That's fine. I'm in the mood for some gnocchi. Suggest Giacomo's to Alfonso. I dig their pasta sauce. Now if you'll excuse me, I'm fucking exhausted."

As I stand up to take my leave, he goes for his phone. Before he dials Alfonso, he says, "I'm proud of you, kid."

"For what?" I used to live to make him proud. I coveted those words. He's given them to me at last, and I'd rather he suffocated on them.

"Embracing your destiny."

"Thanks."

That's it. If I don't leave this room this instant, I'm going to lose my shit. I have to see Jules. I need her in my arms, if only for a minute. She steadies me when I feel unsteady, like a mooring to a ship in a storm. She's my anchorwoman. All my life I've been petrified of letting anyone be that for me, but who wants to go through this dark, terrible world without someone who knows how to hold you together when you feel like you're falling to pieces? She wants the job. She can handle the job. I'm going to give it to her.

Before I hung up with them this morning, Jules's mom insisted on two things: That I call her Maria, and that I save her phone number and use it any time. I love her for both of those things. The second my bedroom door closes, I'm dialing.

I expect Maria to answer, but it's Jules's voice I hear. "Step one complete?"

"Yeah. Are you home?"

"No, still out on good behavior. Teague is staying with us until he's recuperated enough to fend for himself, so Mom's keeping me out for as long as possible. We're at the Pru."

"You're alone with your mom? Can I see you?"

"Yes and yes, please."

"I can be there in twenty."

Shopping malls suck. I'm jittery. More so than usual. I'm not the type of girl anyone is eager to introduce to their parents. Technically, I've already met Maria, though a few phone conversations and once in person while being shot at and hiding for our lives don't really count, do they? This is closer to how parental introductions are supposed to be done, in a chill environment, probably with some alcohol. The food court of the Prudential Center will do.

I spot Jules and her mom through the crowd. They're at a booth with faux leather seats and a black lacquered table near Boston Chowda Company. Maria sees me first, smiles and waves me over. She's warm and inviting in all the ways I imagine a mom to be, which is pretty impressive given the lifestyle we're all accustomed to. Jules doesn't wait for me to approach the table; she gets up and meets me halfway. As I'm watching her saunter toward me, it occurs to me that meeting halfway is more than a metaphor. It's what love is, at its core: Two people with independent wills, with their own ideas and dreams and goals, making space for each other and shaping new dreams and goals together.

I manage to get out the words, "Hi, gorgeous," and then her lips are on mine and her arms are around me, and she's pressed against my chest so hard it's like she's trying to climb inside me. My gaze wanders over to Maria, who's watching us and seems seconds away from tears. I guess a mother knows whose hands are safe for their children. I think my mother would feel that way about Jules. I slide my fingers into her hair and kiss her forehead.

"This has been the worst weekend of my life. I'm so glad you're here," she says.

"Same."

She lets go of her hold on me, takes my hand. "Come say hi to Mom."

Maria stands up to greet me. In the height of awkwardness, I offer her my hand to shake. "Oh, no, sweetie, in this family we hug." I've gone seventeen years without a mother's embrace. I forgot that it feels like coming home. I have to force myself not to cozy into her, as if I were frozen to the bone in the dead of winter and she were a flaming hearth. "Now help us with this food, would you? Our eyes were much larger than our stomachs."

I want to tell her that I'm a terrible New Englander who detests clam chowder, but there's a basket of cheese biscuits calling my name, so I shut up, sit down, and dig in.

The three of us laugh a lot throughout our impromptu early dinner. It's nice to be ordinary for a change. Maria takes the trays topped with trash to the bin and, when she returns, her eyes are on Jules's and my intertwined digits atop the table. "I'm going to pop down to Newbury Street. After the last few days, your father owes me a very expensive tennis bracelet and maybe a necklace to match, don't you agree?"

Jules nods. "He def does. Tiffany?"

"That'll be my first stop, then on to Cartier."

"Oh my God, Mom, I love that for you," Jules replies with a chortle.

I take it as a signal that we're leaving, but Jules stops me. "Mom prefers to shop for jewelry on her own. Some people go to church to have religious experiences; she goes to jewelers."

"Very well put. And won't it be nice to enjoy some 'you time' without Mom around?" She grins. "We'll meet back here in a few hours."

Maria disappears into the crowded food court. "Did your mom just... encourage us to have a quickie?"

Jules laughs until she's out of breath. "No, babe. She's cool but not that cool." She leans in for a kiss, then whispers into my ear. "Why, are you in the mood for one? Because I wouldn't mind getting absolutely railed in the fitting room at Saks." When she moves away, I see that her smirk is downright diabolical. Lustful.

I love that I'm not alone in having nymphomaniacal tendencies. And sex in public places isn't something we do solely out of necessity. She prefers a bed, but she does have a bit of exhibitionism in her. Like me, she finds the possibility of being caught in a compromising position thrilling. It's as if I sensed that in her. We share the same kink, and I'm normally very happy to indulge her, but right now I think the stress of this weekend, compounded by the stress of concocting a plan to dethrone both of our fathers, is weighing so heavy on my shoulders that all I want to do is hold her.

"Is it okay if I'm not? If I want to just sit here in this booth with my arms around you?"

The fire in her eyes is instantly replaced by a mellower glow. Funny how she can switch the devil off and the angel on with such swiftness. She slides her legs up onto the bench, pushes her back into my side, takes my forearms into her hands, and folds herself into me. Head perched against my shoulder, she says, "Cuddlebug Rowan is my favorite Rowan."

I kiss the crown of her head. "Yeah. Turns out I like her, too."

We sit that way as I update her on the situation with the

Rossis, the meal my dad arranged tomorrow night. And then we don't talk much. Two hours pass with me holding her, until Maria returns with a sparkly diamond tennis bracelet on her left wrist.

She shimmies it so the fluorescent light refracts. "Mama's got that brand-new bling. Hold on, have you two been right here where I left you this entire time?"

Jules doesn't move. "Yes."

"I'm not sure when I'll get to see her again after today. I'm trying to fill up on her, I guess."

"Ah, young love." Maria beams. "I remember that."

I walk them to their car. The kiss Jules gives me as we say goodbye is not chaste; I'm aware of her mother's presence as her lips are on mine, and even more so after they're not anymore. All Maria does is let out a small "ha" when she reads my embarrassment. Jules says, "Remember that when you're sitting next to Elisa tomorrow night."

"Possessiveness is cute on you."

"Happy to hear it, 'cause you're mine."

"I am. Completely." I open the car door for her, and she goes a touch pink in the cheeks.

TWENTY-ONE

JULES

I can't stand the sight of my father after what I discovered about him yesterday. The same goes for Teague. He must be aware of something, if not everything. I avoided them last night, but it's well into the afternoon and the rumblings of hunger are making it impossible to continue avoiding them.

I find them at the kitchen table. Always the damn kitchen table. Its clear glass top is the only thing in the room that's translucent, nothing to hide and nowhere to hide it. They're scheming. I can tell because silence blankets the room when I walk in. I don't want to know what they're up to. It's too big, too much. I can't block out the brutality anymore. All I can picture is that box of grenades, those tiny handheld bombs, and where they'll end up—the absolute destruction they'll cause. Will they be used to murder unsuspecting villagers on their way to the local watering hole? Or by insurgents to kill enemy soldiers over manmade borders, or for oil, or for worshipping a different God? To think someone could pull a pin out of something the size of a tennis ball and wipe out an entire room of living souls... It's barbaric.

"Good morning. Or afternoon," Teague says in a joking way that falls flat.

"Don't smile. You look like one of those inbred freaks from *The Hills Have Eyes*."

"Savage burn."

"Yes, 'savagely burned' could also be used to describe your face in its current condition."

"Gimme a break, J. I'm trying," he says to my back as I rifle through the fridge.

Honestly, *what* is he trying to do? Win me over? Get me to trust or even like him again? The odds of a massive meteor striking the earth and extinguishing all life are higher than that happening. He tracked my location, hunted me down, cracked me in the face with a handgun, and, oh yeah, tried to murder the woman I want to spend the rest of my life with. He has no path to forgiveness. I'm a Scorpio. We elevate the art of holding grudges to a science.

I was going to make myself a sandwich, but instead settle for something quick and portable in the form of a pre-packaged yogurt parfait.

"Basic politeness is 'trying' to you. Noted," I reply as I hurry to make my escape.

Dad stops me. "Jules, just a minute. Come sit with us, please."

"Can't. The Red Sox are tied with the Yankees in the ninth." Maybe it's true, maybe it's not. There is a game on but I'm not watching it. Rowan says I hex them—they always lose when I watch.

"Juliet, it's important."

"Fine."

Teague is in my chair. Another thing I begrudge him for. I take the one across from him.

My father runs a hand through his short, sandy hair. It's not like him to be worried over words. "I'm getting older. And my enemies are getting bolder. I'm not going to live forever. You and your mother each have a trust in your name, and those belong solely to you in the event of my death. However, Teague and I have discussed it and, when the time comes, he'll be taking control of my ventures."

Oh no, say it ain't so. "Okay."

"That's it? 'Okay'?" Teague leers at me, his battered eye smaller and more squinty than the other.

It's no great loss. I only wish the dynasty were mine so I could tear it asunder. It would be fitting—a Calloway built it, a Calloway obliterates it. "Yes, Gollum. It's your precious. You want it. I don't."

Dad is caught somewhere between disappointment and satisfaction. "I assumed you wouldn't."

"Great. It's sorted. Can I go?"

He dismisses me with a nod. "Enjoy the game." *He's so clueless he has no idea that I don't fucking like baseball.*

Heading back to the quiet solitude of my room, I wonder if it's possible I can still total the car despite not being in the driver's seat. Indirect saboteurs can be as ruinous as deliberate ones. I go to find my mother, who, like me, has been hiding herself away in this big house lorded over by a sad little man. She hasn't voiced it, but that's how I know she's as disgusted with him as I am.

"Mom, I need to borrow your phone."

"Rowan?"

"Yeah." We've been conspiring via my mother's phantom phone number in case my dad decides to turn on my phone and try to access it. It's not connected to a secondary device, thus it's more secure than sending messages from my iPad.

She switches from her main to her alternate number and I shoot Rowan a text.

Teague has to go, too. He's going to inherit the throne and the cycle will continue.

Rowan texts back pretty quickly.

It won't be a problem. One more body in the room when shit hits the fan. When it's time to toss the bait, bait them both. Teague's eager enough to bite.

I don't make a habit of seeking my mom's approval. But if I ever needed it, it's for this. "Tell me we're doing the right thing."

"We are, darling. It's been a long time coming, and it would have happened eventually, with or without us to nudge it along."

TWENTY-TWO
ROWAN

Giacomo's, 8:00 p.m. That's what my father arranges. I get there five minutes early, ask the host for the table reserved under Rossi. He leads me to a booth set for three in a quiet corner tucked away in the back. I don't like crowds, but I dislike the location of this table more. There's a brick wall to my right, a tall, dark, solid wood partition to my left. It's too secluded and cage-like. *Deal with it.*

Alfonso likes to make people wait. It's a power move he and I both have in our repertoire. I don't care; he can make it. He does have the power in this situation. I've pissed him off, jeopardized his potential for enterprise growth and, worse, hurt his daughter's feelings as well as her pride. While I have no fucks to give about his business, I do have guilt about upsetting Elisa.

I take the liberty of ordering a bottle of chianti for the table and pour myself a glass as I wait: 8:05, 8:10, 8:15. He arrives right on time, in other words fashionably late, with Elisa in tow. He's in a gray suit, no tie. No tie is good: He's not so angry as to view this as an official business meeting, more a casual meal with an associate. Gray is also good: It can't hide bloodstains so he probably, hopefully, isn't itching to put a bullet in my head or anywhere else.

Elisa is in an unfussy black cocktail dress, hair down, makeup understated. Pretty, as always. It's not that I don't find her attractive—I do. Maybe we could've happened organically if our parents would've allowed for it, but being forced, pressured... It was never going to work. Neither love nor connection can be compelled into existence.

I stand up. "Alfonso, Elisa, thank you both for coming." The handshake originated in ancient Greece circa the fifth century BC. Its purpose was to prove to acquaintances, new and old, that you were unarmed and had affable intentions. That's what it means tonight in twenty-first-century Boston, inside this hole-in-the-wall Italian restaurant; I come in peace, please don't fucking gut me like a fish.

He shakes my hand. Practiced as I am at remaining emotionless to the outside world, internally I'm relieved. We all take our seats. I pour him and Elisa a glass of wine, take a huge gulp of mine, then begin. "I owe you both an apology and I mean it, sincerely. I apologize. I meant no disrespect to either of you."

"Not another word," Alfonso says, signaling *stop* with his hand. "I'm too hungry to talk. First, we eat. Then we see if this is reparable." He motions the waiter over without so much as a glance at the menu. As he listens to the night's specials, Elisa looks at me.

"Gnocchi, right?" she asks with a wounded half-smile.

"El, I'm..." No. *I'm sorry* isn't good enough. She deserves an explanation. "Sometimes you meet someone you didn't see coming and the draw is undeniable, too powerful to walk away from, no matter what's at stake. That's what happened between Juliet Calloway and me."

"I'm not upset that you're with someone else. I'm upset that you didn't respect me enough to be honest about it. You let me have more-than-friendly feelings for you when you never felt the same for me."

"I care about you, I do. But you're right, that isn't how you treat someone you care about."

"No, it's not." She shifts her focus to the waiter, gives him her order, and mine. "I get it, though. Love is like shit—it happens."

I bite down on my lip to keep from laughing. "You should put that on a t-shirt. It'll sell like hotcakes, I'm telling ya."

She gives me a wink. I'm happy to receive it.

"Everything cleared up between you?" Alfonso asks his daughter.

"Yeah. We're good."

"Good." He picks up his glass of wine, swills it, and takes a sip. After he swallows, he raises an eyebrow at me. "It would've been a real shame if I had to whack you. We'll sort out the rest after dinner."

The meal is finished; the plates are cleared away. Alfonso orders each of us a shot of sambuca and a serving of tiramisu. I sure as fuck am not going to tell him that I can't stomach the black licorice flavor of anise, so I shoot the shot as God intended— faster than a racehorse that has to take a piss. It's awful, but it's alcohol, and I could use the liquid courage for the gamble I'm about to take.

"Impressive. Would you like another one?" Elisa slides her shot closer to me.

"No, thanks. What I'd like to do is pitch you a business proposal, Alfonso."

He throws his hands up. "Why not? Hit me with it."

"You and my father have an alliance you wanted to solidify via a marriage between Elisa and me. A nice, easy arrangement for the two of you, but this isn't medieval times. Women have agency. We make our own money, we own property, we can inherit wealth, we choose who we marry, and most of us do it for love. I'm not in love with Elisa. I wish I were, she's smart and funny and beautiful, it's that *something extra* that's missing. We've been friends since we were kids and that's always how it was gonna go for us. I think she might tell you the same thing." I consult her.

She nods. "I'd say that's about right."

"There it is. So, no, I'm sorry, we can't consolidate power through marriage. I have something better to offer you. Total control of Boston."

Elisa goes, "What?"

Alfonso leans closer, rests his elbows on the table, and folds his hands. "Total control? How?"

"It's simple, really. I want out. For good. When I take over the family business from my father, I'm taking it strictly legit. I'm going to keep the marina and the yacht club, but everything else my father possesses has to go—the import, export, and domestic businesses, and the service provider contacts for those businesses. If you want them, I'll sell them to you for a reasonable price. Then you'll have all of his assets, none of the competition."

"This is going to happen in my lifetime? And what about Pat Calloway? He's a pain in the ass."

"It's going to happen sooner than you imagine. And Patrick Calloway is not going to continue to be a problem for anyone much longer."

"*Mmm.* The way things have gone to shit so quickly I figured your father would be getting rid of him soon."

Or they'll be getting rid of one another. "I don't know what he has in store for Calloway. I told him I have no interest in any more violence, only the money side of things. In the meantime, until the business changes hands, all you have to do is continue to be our ally. You can't tell me you don't like the idea of being the King of Boston. There's never been an Italian running the underground here. I'm offering you the opportunity to be the first."

Pandering to his vanity and his proud heritage, he's almost sold. I know what's coming out of his mouth next. "How much is it going to cost me?"

"I went over the books this morning. The total value of our current inventory is twenty mil. I'll give it to you for ten. And when the time comes, I'll make sure our service providers are aware of the change in regime."

"Callum knows about all this?"

"He knows I'm going to steer the ship in a different direction, and since I'm his only heir he doesn't have much choice. As far as I'm concerned, I'm being considerate of him by informing him of the future plans for *my* business. You tell me, once he steps down and I'm the admiral, will it matter what my father thinks?"

"No, it won't."

"Then I take it we have a deal?"

"You're a savvy businesswoman. Your dad taught you well. Yeah, we have a deal." We shake on it, which is as close to a written contract as we dare to get in our trade. No tangible evidence. I can't wait for the day when I can leave a paper trail and not worry about getting thrown in jail for it.

"Wait a second." Elisa scrunches her nose at her father. "Does this mean I can't have the Lamborghini you promised me as a wedding present?"

Alfonso pats her hand. "You'll still get your Lambo, *bambina*."

Well, shit, I didn't realize our nuptials were worth a Lamborghini to him. I should've driven up my selling price. "We actually have a Huracán on standby—sky blue, black spoiler. The original buyer backed out."

A low chortle leaches from Alfonso and crescendos to full-blown maniacal glee. He resembles an unhinged Santa Claus, round belly jiggling as he caws. "The benefits of this arrangement keep piling on."

They do, indeed. Sweet freedom is whispering in my ear.

TWENTY-THREE

JULES

Because he's a tech idiot who doesn't know how to turn off the speakerphone once he's inadvertently turned it on, I overhear my father in the kitchen on a call this morning, arranging a shipment for Friday. A man with a thick accent I can't place informs him that a boat will arrive at the wharf at 2 a.m. I'm not sure how much or what kind of product he's moving, but it means two things: His holdings are going to be significantly depleted and a lot of people are approaching their demise. Rowan has to accelerate her timeline. It's a literal matter of life and death.

I have to wait for my mom—and Henry, Dad's goon who's been reassigned to accompany her everywhere, save the bathroom—to get home from the grocery store so I can use her phone. The more sneaking around I have to do to contact Rowan, the more annoyed I become with my father. It's harder than it was in the beginning, when nobody knew about or even suspected us. Now I'm under constant surveillance if I leave the confines of my bedroom. When my dad's out, it's Teague who has his broken nose all up in my grill. *Speak of the devil and he shall appear*.

"Hey." He hobbles into the living room, reaches for something on a high shelf in the tall, recessed bookcase opposite the entertainment center. It's a monumental effort for him. He fails, groans, and rubs at his ribs. I hear him mumble "fuck" and am tempted to help him retrieve whatever it is he's going for. But I'm also getting a sadistic sort of pleasure from watching him writhe. It's like those Japanese game shows where people are pelted with balls as they're trying to accomplish near-impossible tasks. He tries again. Fails again. Fails worse.

For crying out loud. "Yo, Frankenstein, what are you looking for?"

"Uno."

"What?"

"Remember when we were kids? It was our favorite game. Aunt M told me the other day that there's a deck up here somewhere."

"You want to play Uno?"

He signals at my book. "It's not like you got other plans."

Typical. He doesn't ask, he assumes. He's been that way as long as I can remember. I've spent countless hours with him, and I can't recall a single time he's asked me what I wanted to do or see or eat, where I wanted go, how I felt about anything. Is that a guy thing, or is it specific to Calloway men? I've kept quiet, let them discount me. I refuse to do that anymore.

"No, I don't have other plans, but I'm not interested. I'd rather chew on broken glass than hang out with you."

He scowls. "I fucked up, little cousin. I know it. I really fucked up."

Every once and again as I was growing up, I would wish I were a boy. Because then my father would've taught me all the things he didn't want a daughter to know. He valued me, but not the way he does Teague. I'm a possession. Teague is his protégé. Seeing the way Teague turned out, I'm thankful I'm not a boy. I'd be just like him, lowkey misogynistic and myopic.

"Have you ever stopped to wonder about why you hate

Rowan so much? Before the accident with Gino—and that *is* what it was—you hated her. She never did anything to you though, did she? I mean, you've both stayed out of each other's way your whole lives, haven't you? So, what is it? Her name. That's all. You've been made to hate her because of her name. It's pathetic that you're incapable of thinking for yourself, making your own judgments. You're a sheep. A sheep masquerading as a wolf." I go over to the bookcase and grab a deck of playing cards. "Here. Entertain yourself with a few rounds of solitaire."

Mic drop. I don't look back to confirm it, but I know he's standing there with his mouth hanging open. It's dawning on him that he doesn't have to be dead to be dead to me.

I'm hiding in the bathroom with my mom's phone and the shower turned on so I can talk to Rowan in earnest. It's too much information to send via text, and it's too sensitive for it to exist in written words, anyway. I wish I could see her face, but FaceTiming about a coup while we're both in our fathers' homes is unwise.

"Friday. This Friday? That doesn't leave me much time to prepare," she says.

"No."

"Okay. It'll have to be done tomorrow night. It's a rush job, but I'm sure Callum won't hesitate, being the greedy bastard that he is. I'll text you when we're on our way there. You know what to do."

"What do you mean 'we're'? You're not going to be there, are you?" *Oh God, I'm going to throw up.*

"I have to be. I'm back in his good graces since I was able to smooth things over with the Rossis. That doesn't mean he trusts me one hundred percent. He won't think anything of it, as long as I'm putting my own ass on the line right beside his. That's how it works with him."

"I hate this."

"I'll be out of there long before anything happens, I promise. I gotta run, though. I have a call to make."

"You found the right number?"

"Yeah. The ATF has an anonymous tip line."

The ATF is comprised almost exclusively of ignoramuses. Federal agencies take longer to get anything done than it did Moses to lead his people out of the desert to the Promised Land.

"That's—"

"I know what you're thinking. They've been after Callum Monaghan for a long time. All I have to do is drop his name and it'll light a fire under their collective ass."

"That was fast. We've reached the point in our relationship where we can read each other's minds."

Rowan laughs a big, braying laugh. I can picture her, head thrown back, directing the sound of pure joy at the sky. It's the most beautiful sound. "I didn't know that was a real thing. It's a first for me."

"To be your first anything is a pleasant surprise."

"You're my first love. That counts more than any other first."

It takes my breath away how she manages to say the perfect things, regardless of how steeped in sarcasm my words may be. "Oh, I've turned you into a puddle. Do I get a medal or something?"

She clicks her tongue. "I'm hanging up, Juliet."

"Goodbye my darling. Light of my life, moon in my sky."

The line goes dead and I laugh. I take off my shirt, splash some water in my hair—have to make it look convincing—towel it off, and then go find my mom in the second of only two havens she has in this house: The back garden, in which she planted a

plethora of high pollen flowers so that my father, with his aller-
gies, would avoid it. She's too deep into this with us not to be
included on every minute detail, but so adept at duplicity I know
she'll be fine. She's been playing the long game, hiding behind the
façade of dutiful wife and mother for decades. Whatever relief
I'll feel when this is over will be peanuts in comparison to hers.

She sips her iced tea and listens intently as I deliver the
change of plans.

"I know you don't want to hear this," Mom begins, "but it's
good that Rowan will be there. She might be able to limit the
violence. Callum's killer instinct is toned down when she's
around, and the grunts have to take whatever order she gives
them. The poor night guards may live to see sunrise."

"Right. That doesn't do much to abate the nightmarish
visions of my girlfriend being pumped full of lead." It comes out
of my mouth sounding acerbic, but in truth that's all I've seen
lately, whether I'm awake or dreaming—Rowan and my mom
and me, riddled with bullets, the lifeblood leaking out of us
until all that remains is expired meat.

My mom is sporting that knowing air that only mothers
have. The worry extends from her face into her eyes. "After this
is finished, we're going to find you a therapist that specializes in
trauma and PTSD. As much as your father and I have tried to
keep you away from the ugliness of our business, it was
inevitable that some would seep through the cracks."

We're Calloways. We don't do therapy. We don't even step
foot into the confessionals at church. Nobody carries our
burdens for us or hears the slightest breath of our sins; they're
ours and ours alone. No doctor or God can offer us immunity
from real-world repercussions. I'd be better adjusted if I had
been allowed to talk about any of the batshit crazy things I've
experienced in my life. I probably wouldn't be so prone to or
comfortable with lying or manipulating or keeping every
goddamn normal human emotion locked away inside me. And

in the last week, between Gino and Teague and the cemetery, I've seen more carnage than I have in twenty-two years of living.

"Yeah, I think that's a good idea."

I move to hand her back her phone. She shakes her head. "It's yours for now. Keep it hidden from the insufferable men in the house."

"They are barely tolerable, aren't they? Not in the good Elizabeth Bennet kind of way."

"Correct. You're flustered; have a sip of this." She thrusts her glass at me.

The instruction confuses me. I'm not a fan of tea, iced or hot, and she's well aware of that fact. "Mom, I—"

She smirks at the pitcher atop the copper bistro table between us. "It's from Long Island, dear."

"Should've led with that." I help myself to more than a sip.

TWENTY-FOUR

ROWAN

I leave the house to make the call. My dad isn't home, but in true paranoid fashion I worry that every room except the shitter is under surveillance, now that our rivalry with Calloway has boiled over. I choose the patio of Cathedral Station—what must be the only gay sports bar in existence—as my office for the day. *Might as well enjoy a cocktail while destroying everything I know and hate...* And love. I do still have love for my dad, and that's what's making doing the right thing so damn hard. I'm angry at myself for loving him. He's tried everything he possibly could to force me to stop loving him. He's worse than a plague of locusts. But love dies slowly and then all at once. I guess I'm waiting for the "all at once" part to come.

I speak to some low-level ATF intern for no more than thirty seconds. The recipe I concoct has two simple ingredients: I say "Callum Monaghan," add "Patrick Calloway" to the pot, give it a stir, and am transferred to the special agent in charge of the Boston field office. As expected, I am fucking grilled longer than a brisket. I'm asked for the who, what, where, when, why, and how, but I'm not willing to divulge more than is necessary:

There's an arsenal and some bad guys at this location on this time and day, go get 'em.

I lose patience and cut off Agent Whoever-the-Hell. "Christ, man, are you a cop or a journalist?"

"I need to verify that this information is real."

"Show up tomorrow night to the address I gave you and you will. Shit is going to pop off, I guarantee it. But make sure not to bust your nut too quick or they'll scatter like bedbugs when the lights go on."

I hear him suppress a snigger. "It would be helpful if I had your name, at least."

My name. It holds such power. I can get anything I want with my name, move mountains, strike fear into the hearts of big, strong badass men. I wonder if it can summon the full force and fury of the United States government, or if it can save me from them. "I'm... someone close to the Monaghan family."

He either puts me on mute or is rendered speechless. The silence goes on and on. I consider hanging up until he says, "Miss, thank you for the call. Rest assured you'll be treated as an informant and, as such, granted protections under the law."

He's alluding to immunity from prosecution and the witness security program. *Have to catch me first.* I'm not going anywhere, jail or into hiding, unless I want to. "Just be there."

The trap is set. Time to prime the prey. I toss back the rest of my espresso martini and think about ordering another—not because I want one; it's just an excuse to procrastinate. "Fuck it." I slap some money on the table, not bothering to ask for the check.

Jules makes my pitch to my father more believable via pictures of Calloway's holdings. That's what sells him on the idea of ripping him off, more than my words. Upon first glance of them, he goes so bug-eyed I think they might burst right out of their sockets. He's covetous yet still dubious. "Why are you telling me this, and how did you get these?"

"I'm telling you for three reasons: First, things between you and me have never been good, and I want that to change. I was hoping a father–daughter heist might be the thing that does that, you know, since I'm too old to take fishing or play catch with."

He snorts. "What else?"

"Second, Calloway isn't like you. He's controlling, doesn't let his wife or daughter have money or lives of their own. They can't take a shit without their bodyguards. You've been responsible for that all these years, but it's gotten worse since your fucked up assassination attempt on a day of mourning, you psycho." I don't pull my punches because I will forever be seething over it. He averts his gaze from mine. "Anyway, that's also how I got ahold of the pics—Jules gave them to me. She wants out from under Calloway's thumb and figured if we can hit him hard enough, he'll go out of business, then she and her mom will be free of him. I can't be with her, but I haven't stopped loving her and I want to help her if I can. Third, if the Monaghans have that arsenal, we control where it goes. I have no idea who Calloway's selling that shit to, but if I can keep innocent people from being slaughtered like fucking livestock, then I'm going to. Maybe we can do something good for once and sell it to Ukraine. You already ship cars there; you have contacts."

"You're a real bleeding heart, kid."

"Caring about people isn't a weakness. And what do you give a shit, as long as you're making money? You'll make more money from one night's work than you do in a year. And you'll royally screw Calloway without having to murk him. It's a win-win."

He rubs his chin in contemplation. "It is. But tomorrow

night is too soon, and we have a small window. We couldn't move that much product in a couple of hours."

When Callum Monaghan says no, he means no. He didn't say no. There's room for persuasion. I've been watching and learning from Jules, studying her playbook. I'm far from a master manipulator, but taking a small shot at his toxic masculinity might do it.

"So, we fit what we can on a box truck and burn the rest. There're two guards at the door, no cameras, no alarms. You're telling me if we bring in Jeremy, Ryan, and Matthew, the five of us can't handle two guards? Two guards for grenades and Kalashnikovs. C'mon, it's a cake walk. Unless you're afraid or something."

He leans across his desk, intensity radiating throughout his entire being. I got his back up. He has to prove he's got balls. "You calling me a coward?"

"I'm asking if you've finally met a risk you're scared to take. That doesn't make you a coward, it makes you a normal person." If there's anything my father loathes more than being perceived as yellow-bellied, it's being seen as normal. His self-adulation won't allow his crown to be askew.

"Let's put that motherfucker out of business."

Got ya. In roughly thirty-six hours, my life begins anew, sans my father and Calloway. "I'll round up the minions?"

"Do it."

I don't call Jules to let her know it's on. Rather, I wait across the street from her house with my back pressed against an ancient oak tree—using its plush summer leaves and the night as cover—until I see the lights in all the rooms go out one after the other. I've never been inside, but I know her bedroom is on the second floor at the back overlooking the garden. She's told me how much she loves having breakfast on her little stone balcony, watching the kaleidoscope of butterflies that her mom's coneflowers, aster, and zinnia attract.

I approach the black steel fence surrounding the property with an abundance of caution until I'm sure the flood lights mounted on the house aren't automated. Then I lift the latch on the gate and tiptoe the rest of the way down the drive, into the yard.

The soft glow of a bedside lamp lets me know she's still awake. I should find some pebbles to throw at the panes of her French doors, but I'm not in the headspace to be sensible. I'm feeling reckless in my bones. I could die tomorrow night; I've got one last big, romantic gesture in me before I go.

The lattice leading up to her balcony is metal, covered with ivy. "Fuck, I hope it's not the poison variety," I whisper to myself before starting my ascent. I'm not a fan of heights. Never have been. I wouldn't be climbing a goddamn garden trellis for anyone but her.

Hopping over the balustrade to safety feels like the greatest triumph of my life. I fist-bump the air like an idiot, then tap on the doors. They swing open with more ferocity than I expect. Her eyes go wide. She murmurs, "Are you insa—"

I cut her off with a kiss. A desperate one. She deepens it, frees my hair from its ponytail and slides her fingers into it. *Gentle*. Everything about it and her. I don't know how she knows that at this moment I'm so incredibly, terrifyingly fragile inside, but she does.

She doesn't stop kissing me until she's guided me to her bed, and even then, only to disrobe me. She does this gently, too.

Once I'm naked, she sits me at the edge of the mattress and drops to her knees, not bothering to lose a single piece of her own clothing. "Don't take your eyes off mine," she says.

I nod.

She spreads my legs, kisses the entire length of my inner

thighs. And then her tongue is dancing on my slit, relishing the taste of me.

The look in her eyes is so full of love—mellow yet determined—as she takes my clit into her mouth. I move to palm her crown, but she catches my hand, instead lacing our fingers together and pinning our hands to the bed. She starts with light, quick flicks, crescendos the pressure and speed.

Soon, I'm on fire. I'm dying to moan but know I can't. It takes everything I have to keep quiet. I squeeze her hand as my body starts to shake. She slips two fingers inside me, massaging my G-spot.

My orgasm is intense. Roaring. But I'm silent. I collapse onto the mattress and close my eyes as I ride out the waves of chemicals flooding my system.

She doesn't give me much time to recover, just long enough to slip out of her airy nightdress and panties. She pulls me upright and climbs into my lap, wrapping her legs around my torso and her arms around my neck. I feel her wetness on my pelvis. She kisses me again, glides her tongue into my mouth. I slide three fingers into her, deep as they can go.

I concentrate on working the tiny bundle of nerves inside her, palming her ass with my free hand as she grinds her clit against the base of my thumb. She's quieter than she's ever been, but I feel her pulsating around my fingers—my cue to go faster. She bites her bottom lip and digs her nails into my shoulders as she comes.

By the time she's finished, I'm soaked in her. *Soaked*. All the times we've had sex and she's never…

"You're a squirter!" I whisper.

Then she's silent-laughing into my neck so hard that we're both trembling. "Sometimes. You should take me in a bed more often."

"If I survive tomorrow night, I plan to."

"I should get you a towel."

"Absolutely-the-fuck-not. We can air-dry, it's fine."

She kisses me again, then scuttles off me and lies down. "I know you can't stay, but will you hold me for a while?"

"Like you have to ask." I situate myself beside her. We're sticky with sweat and *other* fluids, but none of it matters. All I care about is that she's in my arms, now and again pressing her lips to my neck.

I climb down the trellis at the earliest hint of sunrise. She watches me and I can feel the worry in her gaze. My feet touch the grass and I see her exhale her anxiety.

I love you, she mouths to me.

I love you, too. More than words can say.

———

It's the longest day of my life. I stew in dread until darkness falls at 8:05 p.m. The minions arrive to pick us up shortly after, in an unregistered 12-foot box truck someone did a slapdash job of painting black. As my father and I are heading out the door I prepare myself to compromise my newfound principle.

"I need a gun."

I don't plan to fire it—the optics of the thing are frightening enough.

"What happened to yours?"

"The one I killed a man with? Yeah, that's at the bottom of the Atlantic Ocean."

"Smart girl, getting rid of it."

I didn't do it because it was proof of a crime, douche. "Whatever. Give me your spare." He's predictable. He pulls up his pant leg and yanks his Beretta Nano from its ankle holster. Small but deadly. "Thanks."

· · ·

We approach the pier with our headlights off, rolling the truck over the hoary boards at a snail's pace. The lighting here is garbage. We're well-hidden in the maws of the night. "It's there, at the end." I point at Calloway's building through the wind-screen. My dad parks a hundred yards from the warehouse entrance, and we stake it out in complete silence.

"You were right. I only see two guards. Nice job, kid." My dad gives me a literal pat on the back. I fight my instinct to squirm at the contact.

"Jeremy and I will take care of the guards. Once they're down, move in."

I turn to give Jeremy directions. "We go up there cool and non-threatening, not with guns blazing. I'll take the one with the beard. You've got the other guy. Don't fuck this up and don't kill him if you don't have to."

"Okay."

"Go on three—one. Two. Three." We hop out, making certain to close the doors softly behind us.

Jeremy is a lumbering idiot, not light-footed in the slightest, but he's keeping pace and that's all I can ask of him. As soon as the guards see us, they're on high alert. I use what little femi-ninity I possess to my advantage and give them a wave. "Sorry, is this private property?" I call out to my designated mark. He recognizes that I'm a woman, and even in the faint glow of streetlamps I see his relief. Sometimes sexism does have its advantages: I'm a girl, not a threat. That's the dumbest thing a man can think. We're smaller in stature, but nature has made us cunning in ways men cannot comprehend.

To Jeremy I murmur, "Go."

I have my gun concealed in my palm. I walk straight up to Whiskers and hold it up to his forehead. I am firm and fearless —as far as he can tell. He is shaking, terrified. Perfect. That's the state I need him to be in. I look over to find Jeremy struggling a bit, but he's bigger than the guard. He takes him into a choke-hold and uses brute strength to strangle him into submission.

"Listen carefully," I mutter close to my guy's ear, "I know you have a gun. Hand it over." He complies without protest, and I tuck it into the back pocket of my black jeans. "You're gonna call your employer and very quietly let him know what's going on here. Do it now."

He fishes his phone out of his pocket but is barely able to hold it steady. Patrick is on speed dial. There's one ring, then Calloway's voice. *"What?"*

The guard says in a near whisper, "The warehouse is being robbed."

"How many guys?"

"I don't know."

"I'm coming." Click.

"Good. I'm sorry for this next part." I hit him so hard in the back of the skull with the butt of my gun that he passes out cold. He hits the pavement face first.

My dad drives the truck up to the front of the building. Matt and Ryan jump out and each grab the handles of the huge, tracked doors. They slide open with a metallic groan. Inside, a goldmine of devastation. My father claps his hands together, rubs them triumphantly. "Alright, let's see what we got. Matty, get on that forklift over there. Rowan, there are cans of gas in the back of the truck. Get this place ready to burn."

I retrieve the gas, walk up and down the aisles, pouring the contents of the red plastic canisters on the floors as I go. From the start that was my Plan B: If the cops flake, this place is getting torched. Maybe I'll lock Calloway and my dad inside and watch the fucking joint go up in smoke.

When I'm finished, I shoot a text to Jules. She and Maria have to rile up Patrick and Teague, give 'em some real *ra-ra* cheerleader shit to hype up their manhood.

I stand by the doors, leaning against the wall with my arms

folded. Watching and waiting. The underlings manage to load three pallets of grenades and one pallet of AK-47s into the truck before I hear the rumble of speeding tires on the planks of the pier. That's my cue to find cover. I sneak to the rear of the warehouse, duck behind a towering pallet.

Outside, car doors slam. One, two, three. "I fucking knew it would be you, Monaghan!" Calloway shouts.

And then there are no more words, only the earsplitting *crack-crack-crack* of handguns as they release bullets.

Then, sirens. Blue and red flashing lights cutting through the darkness of the warm summer night, reflecting off the inner walls of the warehouse. The pistols fall silent, replaced by a deep voice through a megaphone. I glance around my pallet in time to catch Calloway's men and my dad's men placing their weapons on the ground. I don't see Calloway, but my father is lying motionless just beyond the wide-open warehouse doors, his blood oozing out of him and pooling around his head. *It was a headshot. It had to be.*

I knew I'd feel something when this day came, although I didn't expect that the world would suddenly be moving in slow motion. I slink closer to my father's body, careful to stay out of sight and well-hidden by crates. It feels like miles of hard, sluggish trudging through a swamp of grief. I'm aware of ATF agents cuffing Matt and Ryan and Jeremy, and Teague, the two guards, and a few other guys I don't know, but all I can focus on is Callum Monaghan, dead on the weather-battered, splintering pine boards. I'm close enough to see that his eyes are cold, lifeless orbs forever focused on the sky. I hope the stars imprinted on his cones and rods as he faded away. That would've been a comfort he didn't deserve; I wish for it, nonetheless.

I have tears for him. Another thing I hadn't expected, but they splash down my cheeks—droplets at first and then a steady stream. I wipe them away with my fingertips. "You stupid, selfish, insatiable man," I whisper aloud, in case his soul is still lingering. The only thing that could've allayed his greed was his demise.

Incoherent screaming demands my attention. Teague, arms cuffed behind his back, rears against the agent escorting him to an ATF vehicle. I see what he sees—Patrick Calloway bent backward over a rusted guardrail, his top half peppered with bullet holes. I have tears for him, too. How tragic and poetic, two kings killed by one another—destined to be each other's downfall. These violent delights have violent ends. They always do.

I have to go look into Jules's eyes and tell her that her father is dead. She shouldn't learn of it any other way. Agents will be coming in to start cataloging soon. I don't want to be here when that happens.

I make my way to the blue-gray door at the rear of the warehouse, away from the commotion and the cops, the gore and the corpses. I think I'm clear until, "Stop right there!"

Of course, I don't stop. I don't even bother to turn around. I run. I hear footsteps chasing after me, commands being yelled, the hissing static of two-way radios. Outside in the narrow alley, I'm converged on from all sides. Ahead of me is the end of the pier. This is it.

There is no escape.

There's one.

It's suicide.

Or freedom.

Freedom, either way—just two different kinds.

I climb the guardrail, take a breath, and hurtle feet-first off the pier. On my way down I pray. I close my eyes as I splash into the Charles River. The water is warm, and mercifully neither rocky nor shallow. I kick my way up to the surface, float on my back, and let the current carry me downstream into Boston proper.

TWENTY-FIVE

JULES

Anxious is not the correct word for what I'm feeling. There isn't a sole comprehensive word: Jittery, fretful, anticipating the worst. I'm not the type of person who believes in much of anything preternatural. Not God, ghosts, or clairvoyance. If there were a God, the planet wouldn't be in such a woeful state of decay. I mean, you'd think an all-powerful creator would take some pride in their creation and intervene, right? If there were ghosts, we'd have tangible, verifiable documentation—photos, videos, a hundred witnesses to corroborate one instance of inter-action. If divination were real, there wouldn't be countless deaths from disasters because someone, somewhere would see them coming and we'd be able to prepare. Tonight, I believe in intuition. My intuition is telling me that someone, or multiple people, will not be among the living come daybreak.

It's not intuition though, is it? It's scientific. I've observed vicious men do vicious things. I've narrowly escaped said things with my life. Time and time again they themselves narrowly escaped with their lives. That's pattern recognition. My general conclusion is that tonight is the night some of those men see their luck run out.

My mother is calm. How she's maintaining her calmness, I'm uncertain. She's aided by a stiff drink and a mindless reality TV show. My stomach is churning; I'll regurgitate alcohol in a hot minute, so that's off the table for me. *I wish I had some weed.*

"*Topolina*, you do realize you're pacing, yes?"

"Thank you, Mother, how very astute."

She huffs. "It helps if you can talk yourself into believing that there is nothing you can do. Whatever happens, happens. It is what it is, and you can't control or fix the outcome. That's the plain truth of it."

I'm not good with uncertainty. I like plans and lists and over-preparedness. I thrive when I can predict every possible outcome. And... "I hate waiting." It's too easy to start spiraling when I have too much time to think. I've had hours. My mother's sage words offer no comfort.

The doorbell rings and I'm so startled by it that I nearly molt my skin. I bolt to it, opening to find Rowan on the other side, sopping wet from head to toe. I force her through the doorway and into my arms.

"I'm getting you wet." She tries to push me away.

I hold on. "I don't care."

"Rowan, sweetheart, why do you look like a drowned cat?" My mother's entrance into the hallway pulls us apart.

"I went for a swim in the Charles. It would've been lovely if I didn't do it to escape the Feds."

Mom goes to retrieve a towel from the linen closet. In addition to being soaked, Rowan seems... haunted. Shell-shocked, perhaps. I can't know what she witnessed—she wouldn't let me be there with her despite my begging—but I do know it was ugly.

Mom returns with a towel and also a change of clothes—gray silk pajamas. "Go dry off, get changed, then come tell us what happened."

. . .

We three sit on the couch. Rowan doesn't speak right away. She has a lot to say but can't find the words she needs. I hold her hand as the cogs in her brain turn, soundlessly reassuring her that she is not alone and won't ever be again. Calloway, Monaghan, whatever. She is the family I've chosen.

"I don't know who... I didn't see what happened," she begins. "I heard Patrick's car pull up and I hid behind some stacked boxes. There was shooting. Two guns, at least, maybe more. The cops broke it up." She takes a breath. Her voice cracks. "Um... My dad is dead, and Patrick is, too. I think they killed each other. I had to leave them there like that or else I'd be on my way to prison with everyone else. I'm so sorry. First, I hid like a coward, and then I ran like a coward."

"You're not a coward, you're a survivor. You came back to me like you promised," I reply, before realizing that there may be some validity to intuition after all. I'm not shocked that Patrick Calloway is dead. I'm sad for the loss of my father, of course, but—terrible as it sounds—I'm unfazed by the loss of the man he was outside these walls. The world is safer without him in it. Still, I cry for him. Through the torrent I see that my mother is crying, too. She takes my other hand.

"Teague's okay," Rowan adds after a while, as she stares into the distance at nothing in particular. "He was arrested, but he's alive. I don't know what happens next... Not to sound crass or cold, it's just something I thought of. I'm pretty sure the government will try to seize our assets if they treat this like a RICO case—the stuff they can trace in Patrick and Callum's names, anyway."

"We'll lose some things, but we'll still have plenty," my mom says to me. "We have a good lawyer and the trusts in our names are offshore. Your dad had the foresight for that. Plus, there's the *other* thing."

"What about Rowan?" I ask. To Rowan, I say, "You could marry me. Then I can put your name on whatever it is I still own, and you'll never have to worry about finances. Legally, everything will be half yours." It's not the most romantic thing I've said in my life. It's practical.

Rowan flashes an unconvincing smile. "I'll be okay. I'm always okay." She cups my cheeks in her hands and kisses my forehead. "I am going to marry you someday. Not for money, for love."

I don't doubt that. Everything she's done in her life, good or bad, she's done for love.

TWENTY-SIX

ROWAN

FIVE MONTHS LATER...

I'm used to winter in Boston. It's not that different in Spokane—significantly less snow, which is nice—but the early December temps are similar. It's warm enough today to have the windows cracked in my Rogue. Nissan... I didn't think I'd like it, but it's nice. Reliable. It suits my needs. Besides, I never did get my Jeep back. I didn't want it back—too many reminders of my old life attached to it.

I have a job out here as a bank teller. I'm pretty sure I only got it because Alistair is charming and very good at bullshitting. He did me a solid, pretending to be my ex-boss at a Salem Five Bank branch in Boston. It's not a bad job; it requires basic math skills, patience, and a friendly smile. The constant smiling is the hardest part for me. Being immersed in the real world, I'm finding that people in general, not just mobsters, are unpleasant if not entirely douchey. Handling money doesn't intimidate me whatsoever, with the wads of cash I used to deal with.

I don't need to work; I want to. Dad died; there were no charges brought against him. Turns out the government doesn't like to waste time or money prosecuting corpses. And since there's no longer a tyrant to serve, the Monaghan crime syndicate pretty much dissolved itself, which was a good thing not only for me, but Alistair and Ben. They're back in Boston, still looking over their shoulders, but the threat dies down with each passing day. Dad's legal, squeaky-clean business—the marina—is mine, plus all the shit he had stashed there that was not above board. As agreed, I kept the marina—Al and Ben are running it for me—and sold the trash to Alfonso Rossi. I have ten million dollars I don't want sitting in a bank account in the Cayman Islands. I'll leave it for our kids—if we have any—and they won't know it's blood money. I say "if" but, knowing Jules, she'll want at least two. That's my magic number, too. Nobody should grow up without a sibling to bitch about their parents with.

I bang a right onto Sharp Ave and head for what Jules calls the Mess Hall—the student center—not because they serve food there, but because it's where you get to see how stressed out and overwhelmed college kids are all of the time.

The campus is almost deserted this close to the semester's end. I spot Jules sitting on a bench, shivering like one of those tiny, high-strung dogs despite her parka and all the layers she's wearing beneath it. She walks around to the passenger side and slides in.

"Hi." She leans across the center console for a kiss. I am more than happy to oblige her.

As she buckles her seatbelt I ask, "Why didn't you wait inside, you adorable crazy person? I know you're cold, it's below sixty." I roll up the windows and blast the heat, then take off toward the airport.

"I just spent two hours in a stuffy room taking an exam. I needed some fresh air."

"Speaking of which, congrats! Last exam of your college career. How do you feel?"

"I don't know. Scared, like life starts right this second and

I'm completely unprepared for it. I don't have a job lined up yet and I'm..." She drops her words in favor of a sigh.

I know she's stressing about the future, even though she doesn't need to work any more than I do. Everything in her father's warehouse was seized by the ATF, but they couldn't touch her parents' house and couldn't find all of her dad's money. It's about outrunning our legacies and making new ones for ourselves. I scoop up her hand and kiss the back of it.

"Well, I am wicked proud of you. And you should be proud of yourself. Let's worry about the rest when we get back from Boston, okay? I'm actually kind of excited to have a real Christmas, with a tree and twinkly lights and presents." All that stopped when my mom passed away.

"I told my mom how much you like Christmas and how shitty your dad always was about it, so she had the entire house decorated by a professional for you."

That's sweet but kind of excessive. "What?"

"Yeah."

"She paid someone to put up a tree and string lights. That's a thing? Like, an actual profession?"

"Apparently. My dad, Teague, and I used to do it until I went away for school, then it was Dad and Teague's thing." A subtle frown makes itself at home on her face. I forget sometimes that she had happy moments with her father. Moments when he was Patrick Calloway, regular dad and uncle who loved his daughter and nephew.

"Do you want to visit Teague while we're home?"

She's not ready to admit it, but she misses him. After months of working on "forgiveness and creating healthy boundaries" in therapy, she's started taking his phone calls. That's pretty significant.

"No," she says firmly. "Orange isn't his color."

Unfortunate, since he's going to be wearing it exclusively for the next ten years. His new home is the Federal Correctional Institution in beautiful downtown Berlin, New Hampshire. I do feel bad about that, considering I should be locked up, too. I got lucky. He didn't. I remind myself that he's better off inside than out. He has three hots, a cot, and he's enrolled in college classes. He might take something positive away from his incarceration that he wouldn't have bothered trying for otherwise.

"Thought I'd pitch the idea, is all."

"It was a wild pitch, darling." She throws a glance over her shoulder to the back seat for dramatic effect. "Oh wow, you managed to fit all the stuff in the trunk. I'm impressed."

"I'm good at packing. It's like real-life Tetris. I still don't see why you felt the need to bring half your wardrobe for a two-week trip."

"We have four different holiday parties to attend, and Rose's is the event of the season. You can't expect me to plan an outfit for each one so far in advance. Anyway, it's very sexy that you're so efficient. Look at all that space back there!" She chortles, then bites her lip. "I have an idea. We've got three hours before our flight. Want to find a place to park and have a semi-public quickie for old times' sake?"

Hell yes, I do. I love having an apartment with a huge, comfortable bed for us to have sex in, but it's called a "kink" for a reason. "We're coming up on the Arboretum. I do believe that would be a very nice place to park."

"Did you pack your strap-on? I'm in the mood."

"Who are you talking to right now? I even made sure it was easily accessible."

There's that devilish grin she wears so well. She takes my hand from the gearshift and glides her fingers into the spaces between mine. "Let's go."

A LETTER FROM KRISTEN

Dear reader,

I want to say a heartfelt thank you for choosing to read *Forbidden Girl*. If you enjoyed it and want to keep up to date with all my latest releases, just sign up at the following link. Your email address will never be shared, and you can unsubscribe at any time.

www.bookouture.com/kristen-zimmer

I hope you loved *Forbidden Girl* and, if you did, I would be very grateful if you could write a review. It makes such a difference helping new readers to discover one of my books for the first time.

I love hearing from my readers – you can get in touch through social media.

Thanks,

Kristen

facebook.com/authorkristenzimmer
x.com/kristen_zimmer
instagram.com/kristen_zimmer_author

ACKNOWLEDGMENTS

As always, a huge and heartfelt thank you to my literary agent, Mark Falkin, who refuses to quit on me even when I want to quit on myself.

To my tag-team of stellar commissioning editors, Jessie Botterill and Natalie Edwards, as well as the rest of the Bookouture publishing team: I am eternally grateful to you for your guidance, patience, and all the hard work you do.

Mom, Dad, Grandpa, Breanna, and Liz: I owe you all so much for your undying belief in and support of my silly, wild writing dreams. I love you guys.

PUBLISHING TEAM

Turning a manuscript into a book requires the efforts of many people. The publishing team at Bookouture would like to acknowledge everyone who contributed to this publication.

Audio
Alba Proko
Sinead O'Connor
Melissa Tran

Commercial
Lauren Morrissette
Hannah Richmond
Imogen Allport

Cover design
Mary Luna

Data and analysis
Mark Alder
Mohamed Bussuri

Editorial
Natalie Edwards
Sinead O'Connor

Printed in Great Britain
by Amazon

44735152R00128